GIRL,
STOLEN

GIRL, STOLEN

April Henry

Christy Ottaviano Books
Henry Holt and Company
New York

Henry Holt and Company, LLC
Publishers since 1866
175 Fifth Avenue
New York, New York 10010
www.HenryHoltKids.com

Library of Congress Cataloging-in-Publication Data
Henry, April.
Girl, stolen / April Henry.—1st ed.
p.   cm.
"Christy Ottaviano Books."
Summary: When an impulsive carjacking turns into a kidnapping, Griffin, a high
school dropout, finds himself more in sympathy with his wealthy, blind victim,
sixteen-year-old Cheyenne, than with his greedy father.
ISBN 978-0-8050-9005-5
[1. Kidnapping—Fiction.   2. Blind—Fiction.   3. People with disabilities—Fiction.
4. Carjacking—Fiction.   5. Fathers and sons—Fiction.]   I. Title.
PZ7.H39356Gir 2010   [Fic]—dc22   2009050781

First Edition—2010
Printed in August 2010 in the United States of America by R. R. Donnelley & Sons
Company, Harrisonburg, Virginia

1   3   5   7   9   10   8   6   4   2

For Sadie, who showed me our shadows walking backward

GIRL,
STOLEN

A Thousand Things Wrong

Cheyenne heard the car door open. She didn't move from where she lay curled on the backseat, her head resting on her bent arm. Despite the blanket that covered her, Cheyenne was shivering.

She had begged her stepmom to leave the keys in the car so she could turn on the heat if she got cold. After some back-and-forthing, Danielle had agreed. That had only been five minutes ago, and here she was, already back. Maybe the doctor had phoned in the prescription and Danielle hadn't had to wait for it to be filled.

Now the door slammed closed, the SUV rocking a little as weight settled into the driver's seat. The engine started. The emergency brake clunked as it was released. The car jerked into reverse.

It was a thousand little things that told Cheyenne something was wrong. Even the way the door closed hadn't sounded right. Too fast and too hard for Danielle. The breathing was all wrong too, speeded up and harsh. Cheyenne sniffed. The smell of cigarettes. But Danielle didn't smoke and, as a nurse, couldn't stand anyone who did.

There was no way the person driving the car was her stepmom.

But why would someone else have gotten in the car? It was a Cadillac Escalade, so it wasn't likely someone had just gotten confused and thought it was their car.

Then she remembered the keys. Somebody was stealing the car!

And Cheyenne was pretty sure they didn't know she was in it.

She froze, wondering how much the blanket covered her. She couldn't feel it on the top of her head.

Cheyenne felt like a mouse she had seen in the kitchen one time when she turned on the light before school. Caught in the middle of the floor, it had stood stock-still. Like maybe she wouldn't notice it if it didn't move.

But it hadn't worked for the mouse, and now it didn't work for Cheyenne. She must have made some small sound. Or maybe the thief had looked back to see if someone was following and then realized what the shape was underneath the blanket.

A swear word. A guy's voice. She had already halfway known that it was a guy, the way she sometimes just knew things now.

"Who the hell are you?" His voice broke in surprise.

"What are you doing in Danielle's car?"

Their words collided and tangled. Both of them speaking too fast, almost yelling.

Sitting up, she scrambled back against the door, the one farthest from him. "Stop our car and get out!"

"No!" he shouted back. The engine surged as he drove faster.

Cheyenne realized she was being kidnapped.

But she couldn't see the guy who was kidnapping her or where they were going.

Because for the last three years, Cheyenne had been blind.

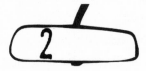

Drawing Blood

The girl in the backseat wouldn't stop yelling. She had black hair and huge brown eyes, wide with fright. Maybe she was pretty. Griffin didn't know. All he knew was that right now she was a big problem. Even though he was freaking out, he forced himself to think. Thank God no one was nearby.

If he stopped and let her out, the way she kept demanding, this girl would run screaming to the first person she saw. In ten minutes or less, he would be arrested. And then the cops would naturally drive out to their house, and everything would unravel. All of them in jail. Probably for a long time.

Instead of slowing down, Griffin accelerated as he turned out of the far end of the parking lot. It threw the girl off balance. He winced as her head clunked against the window, but still he kept going. He was acting on pure instinct now. And instinct told him to get as far away as possible. Growing up around Roy, you got pretty good at running. Running and hiding.

Griffin caught a break, hitting a gap in traffic. He drove as fast as he could across the freeway overpass. The Escalade leaped forward when he pressed the accelerator, hitting sixty-five with no sign of strain.

With the way today was going, the cops would pull him over for speeding. Griffin needed time to think this through, but there was no way he could afford to take it. He figured he had to put as much distance as he could between whoever had been driving this car and the girl in the backseat, who must belong to them. To get away from any witnesses who might be calling 9-1-1 on their cell phones right now. Cutting in front of a red Honda, he took the next corner on two wheels, getting off the main road.

He pounded the side of his head in frustration. How could he have been so stupid as to not notice that there was someone in the car? Griffin could hear Roy shouting at him, almost as real as the girl in the backseat, the girl who wouldn't stop yelling.

He hadn't been able to see past the keys dangling in the ignition. It was that simple, and that senseless. Griffin had been walking down the long rows of vehicles, looking like any other stressed-out Christmas shopper who couldn't find his car. Instead, he was looking for packages he could boost. The packages came from the big, boxy stores that surrounded the acres and acres of the shopping center's parking lot. (The whole place was so big that most people left one store, got in their cars, and drove the equivalent of three blocks to the next store.)

Thanks to Roy, Griffin knew how to get in and out of a locked car in under a minute. He could do it even when someone was climbing out of the next car, and they wouldn't notice a thing. Sometimes, just for a thrill, Griffin would even give a nod as he straightened up with the J. Crew bag or the box from Abercrombie. Then he would stroll down to his own car, parked near one of the exits, and put the bags in the trunk. After the trunk was full, he would drive into Portland and across the river to Eighty-second Avenue, where any of a string of secondhand stores was happy to buy new merchandise for resale, no questions asked.

The Escalade had been a gift, a surprise present meant just for him. Anyone who was stupid enough to leave the keys dangling from the ignition, in full view of the world, deserved to have the car taken away. And he couldn't wait to bring it home and present it to Roy.

That's what Griffin had thought, anyway, until the blanket in the backseat turned out to have a girl underneath it.

Ignoring the girl, ignoring his own panicked thoughts, the explanations and rationalizations he was already practicing for when he got back home, Griffin drove as fast as he could without losing control. Too fast for her to risk jumping out. He kept his head half turned, one eye on the road and the other on her. Weaving around slower cars, Griffin took a side street, and then another, until finally he was on an empty road that cut through a piece of scrubland. On each corner, a big white sign advertised it for sale to any interested developers.

As soon as he slowed down, the girl came at him, outstretched hands curved into claws, screaming like a banshee. Her head was cocked to one side, and her eyes were wide and staring. She looked crazy. Maybe she was.

Throwing the car into park, Griffin tried to deflect her, raising his shoulder and turning his head. At least no one was around to hear her. Her fingernails raked down his right cheek, and he could feel she had drawn blood.

He had to do something, but what? He squeezed between the seats. Griffin just wanted her to calm down, but he ended up wrestling with her, both of them struggling in a desperate silence. Finally, he managed to straddle her and pin her arms to her sides. He was bigger than she was, and he was working on pure adrenaline. At least she had stopped screaming. The sound of their ragged breathing filled the car. He became aware of a quiet hum—he had never had time to turn off the car. Straightening up, he managed to quickly reach over and turn off the key.

"I'm sorry," he said into the complete silence. "Let's talk about this. But you have to promise that you'll stop trying to kill me."

"I will." She nodded, her eyes not meeting his. Griffin

figured she was probably lying. In the same situation, he knew he would lie.

He exhaled. "Look, it's an accident you're here. I just wanted the car, not you. I didn't even know you were in the car."

"Then let me go." Her voice was low and hoarse. She took a deep breath and then started to cough, a deep, racking sound. She kept her head turned away, but still little flecks of spit landed on him. When she spoke again, it was in a whisper. "Please, please, just let me go. I won't tell anyone."

Even Griffin wasn't that dumb. "I'm sorry, but do you think I really believe that? By the end of the day, my description would be handed out to every cop and broadcast on every radio station in town."

A strange expression played across her face, the ghost of a smile. In the cold, the engine ticked as it cooled. "But I won't be able to tell them anything. Didn't you notice that I'm blind?"

Blind? Griffin stared at her dark eyes. He had thought they weren't really meeting his because she was looking past him for help, searching for a way out, assessing the situation.

"You're really blind?"

"My cane's on the floor."

Still wondering if she was tricking him somehow, he looked on the floor. Sitting next to a small black purse behind the driver's seat was a folded bundle of white sticks.

Griffin imagined doing what she asked. He could let her get out. Maybe give her her cane, maybe not. She could probably hear cars okay, and it wasn't like there were a lot of them. Instead of getting run over, she would flag down the next vehicle that came along. But as soon as someone stopped for her, it wouldn't be long until the police were involved. The brand-new Escalade didn't exactly blend in. What if someone passed by here only a minute or two after he let her go? He was thirty miles from home, thirty miles from where he could hide the car. It would be all too easy to track him down. And after that, it was still the same nightmare scenario. All of them locked up and the key thrown away for good.

No. Better to keep her for a little while yet. Ask Roy what to do, even though he wouldn't be happy about Griffin bringing back trouble. Better to bring it back than to leave it out here, ready to explode and engulf them all in the fallout. Besides, Griffin already had an idea. Tonight, after it got dark, he could drive this girl someplace deserted and let her out and then drive away again. Leave her someplace where it would be hours before anyone found her. Just like she asked, only with a lot less chance of being caught. But not here. Not now. Not in daylight. Not when a car might come by at any moment.

As if to make the thought real, he heard a car in the distance. Approaching them.

"I can't let you go," he said, and was starting to add,

"not right now," but before Griffin even got the next word out of his mouth she was fighting him again, opening her mouth to scream. What could he do? Then he had an idea. He didn't know if it would work, but he had to do something. Desperately, he groped across the passenger seat until his fingers closed on what he needed.

Griffin pressed the barrel against her temple.

"Shut up or I'll shoot you."

Every Reason to Lie

Cheyenne froze at the touch of the cold metal. She could tell that he meant what he said. He sounded angry and out of control, just like she felt. They were both quiet until the car passed them and the sound of its engine faded. She could feel her strength draining away with it.

"Look—can't you just chill?" His voice sounded a little calmer.

She made herself nod.

"I don't need this crap. I don't need you screaming and kicking and scratching. I can't think when you do that. So are you going to be quiet?"

Cheyenne nodded again, wishing she could curl up into a tighter and tighter ball, grow smaller and smaller until she just disappeared.

"I *am* going to let you go," he insisted.

Something must have flickered on her face, betrayed her doubt.

"I *am*! Just not now. Right now, I'm going to have to tie you up and cover you with the blanket so that no one can see you. And tonight, once it's dark, I'll let you go."

Her head ached where it had slammed against the window. That had probably only been five minutes ago, but it felt like a lifetime. Where were they now that he felt he could hold her down in the backseat without anyone noticing? That lone car had been the only one she had heard since he had turned onto this road.

"Take off your shoes." Cheyenne thought he was trying to stop her from running away, until he added, "And pull out the laces."

She did as he asked, wondering where the gun was pointing. At her head, at her heart? Or had he already set it down? The tiny slice of blurry vision she had left didn't reveal any clues. He ordered her to lie down on her side, facing the seat, then tied her hands together behind her. Cheyenne knew he couldn't be holding the gun when he did that, but even so, he could still pick it up and shoot her if she gave him any trouble. She did as he asked, but at the same time tensed her wrists and held them as far apart as she dared. With the second shoelace, he tied her ankles together. Why couldn't she have worn loafers?

Her mind raced. When he was finished, she rolled over so that she was facing him. She wanted him to see her face, to see her eyes even if she couldn't see his. It would probably be easier to shoot someone in the back.

She didn't want to make it easy for him.

Cheyenne heard him pick up her purse and begin to rummage through it.

"Are you looking for money?" she said. "Because I don't have much."

Cheyenne knew she had a twenty, two tens, and some ones. The twenty was folded the long way, the ten the short way, and the ones weren't folded at all. Whenever she got money back from someone else, she asked which bill was which and then folded it. Every blind person had their own way of folding money to tell it apart. Coins were a lot easier. Each was a different diameter and thickness, and some had smooth edges and some didn't. Even before the accident, when a coin fell to the floor, Cheyenne had been able to tell what it was, just by the sound it made.

Now she offered him a bargaining chip. "I do have an ATM card. Let me go, and I'll give you my PIN. I've got over three thousand dollars in my account."

"Three thousand dollars?" There was something about his voice that made Cheyenne think he was younger than she had first thought. He sounded incredulous.

She dared to let herself hope. "You can have all of it. I don't think you can get more than a thousand out at a time, but I won't tell them that you have the card. I swear."

"I don't want your money!" There was a strange tone to his voice. It was almost like he was hurt by her accusation, which didn't make any sense. It was okay to steal a car, it was okay to kidnap her, but it wasn't okay to take her money? "I'm looking in your purse for something to gag you with."

"You can't. I'm really sick. If you gag me, I won't be able to breathe." It wasn't a lie, but it wasn't the whole truth, either. But if he gagged her, it would make it that much less likely that she would be able to get help.

Cheyenne was shaking, partly with fear, and partly, she thought, because her temperature must be spiking again. It had been one hundred and two in the doctor's office. Dr. Guinn had prescribed antibiotics and said Cheyenne would be all done with them by Christmas. Now the thought struck like a blow to the stomach. *Will I be alive to see Christmas at all?* "That's why we were at the shopping center, so my stepmom could pick up my prescription at the pharmacy. If I can't breathe through my mouth, I'll smother."

He hesitated for a long time. Finally he said roughly, "Promise you won't scream?"

"I promise." Why should either of them believe the other? Cheyenne wondered bleakly as he pulled the blanket over her. They had no reason to tell the truth and every reason to lie. Which meant that he could be planning to hurt her, to chain her up in his basement for years, to shoot her in the heart. Just like she was thinking about how to get away, to get someone's attention, to hurt him so bad that he couldn't hurt her back. There was no point in either one of them trusting the other.

Even though he had pulled the blanket over her head as well as her body, the kidnapper had arranged it so it didn't cover her face. Good. She could still breathe. And because he could see her face, he would remember she was a person, not a long bundle like a rolled-up carpet. It would be a lot easier to shoot a rolled-up carpet. She heard him climb back into the front seat and then the car started.

Cheyenne tried to figure out the direction the car was heading, but she had lost track in the first few minutes after he stole it. All she knew was that the road was quiet and that couldn't be good for her. Quiet meant no one to notice. Quiet meant he could kill her or do whatever he wanted and no one would know. Her thoughts became darker. Danielle and her dad would be called in to identify her body. What would this man do after she was dead? Would he leave her body in the car and abandon both on some logging road that no one would venture down until spring? Or tumble her out into a ditch in the countryside? Or bury her in a shallow grave in the mountains?

The only thing that might save her life was the fact that she couldn't describe what he looked like.

But if Cheyenne couldn't see, how could she escape?

Who's in Charge Now?

Griffin turned the key in the ignition and drove away, still feeling amazed. He started to push the cigarette lighter back into the console, but then stopped and put it in his pocket. He might need it again. He had been afraid that the girl might try to shove his hand away when he threatened to shoot her. Instead she had frozen with fear.

The fact that she had really believed the car's lighter was a gun made Griffin feel oddly powerful. Like he could just wish and make it so.

When music started playing behind him, he almost drove off the road. Then he realized it was a cell phone playing the first few notes to a popular song. After pulling over, Griffin reached back for her purse. He looked in the phone's window that showed caller ID. "It says Danielle Wilder," he said. "Who's that?"

"My stepmom." She gave him what he guessed she

thought was a friendly smile. It was more like a dog baring its teeth. "Let me talk to her and it will buy you some time. I'll tell her she parked in a different row than she thinks. She was in a hurry when she went into the drugstore. It will keep her looking for a few more minutes."

"I don't think so," Griffin said, and watched the fake smile fall from her face like a plate from a shelf. He pressed the power button on the phone until the display dwindled and went black. But even with the power off, could the police somehow trace the phone? He slid the window down and threw the cell phone as far as he could, where it landed in a tangle of blackberry bushes. Too late, he remembered his fingerprints would be on it. He had taken off his gloves to tie her up and then neglected to put them back on again. He swore under his breath. Stupid, stupid, stupid. He was just as dumb as Roy always said. Why couldn't he ever think things through? Feeling his pulse thrumming in his temples, Griffin tried to reassure himself that it would be all right. No one would find that phone for years.

He pulled back onto the road. When he came to a fork, he took a back way that wound between fields. Here the houses were miles apart. He got a cigarette out of his shirt pocket and flicked his lighter.

"You are *not* going to smoke in my stepmom's car!"

"What?" He was half amused, half angry. Didn't she realize who was in charge now?

"First of all, I'm sick. I can barely breathe as it is.

Second, my stepmom will kill you if you stink up her car."

Griffin snorted. But he took the cigarette out of his mouth and put it and the lighter back in his shirt pocket.

For a long time, the car was absolutely silent except for the ragged sound of the girl's breathing. After about fifteen minutes, he saw a car approaching them. As it got closer, he tensed. Would she try to signal somehow, maybe press her feet against the window, or heave herself up so that her face appeared? He angled the rearview mirror so he could look at her. He watched her face tense and could tell she was weighing her options, the same as he would have in her place. But there weren't many. The car passed without incident. The driver was an older man talking on a cell phone. Griffin doubted that the Escalade had even registered on his consciousness.

Her voice, coming from under the blanket, made him jump. "What's your name?"

"What? Are you serious? Do you really think I would tell you that?" He countered with, "What's your name?" For a second, Griffin thought of what it must be like to be her. To be blind. Like being on an amusement park ride in the dark, one of those rides where skeletons jumped out at you or ghosts glided up behind you and you only knew they were there when they wailed in your ear.

"It's Cheyenne," she said softly. "Cheyenne Wilder."

"Why did your parents name you Cheyenne?" Griffin

asked as they drove past two horses—one brown and one black—running free. His eyes followed them for a moment. "Isn't that an Indian tribe?"

"I'm one-thirty-second Indian. Not enough to really matter."

High cheekbones, dark hair, dark eyes—he could see it. His panic had eased a little. "How old are you?" he asked. It was hard to tell. Fourteen? Eighteen? She was smaller than him, maybe five two, and not wearing any makeup, but she also seemed self-assured. Maybe you had to grow up fast if you were blind.

"Sixteen."

"How come you're blind?"

Instead of answering, Cheyenne shifted and changed the subject. "Where are you taking me?"

He shook his head, forgetting again that she couldn't see him. Then he said, "I can't tell you that."

"Well, then, how long until we get there?"

"When we do." An odd flash of memory, some vacation with his parents. His dad just drove, never taking his eyes off the road and never answering Griffin's questions. His mom turned around in the seat and talked to him, snuck him little snacks. They had played games, like spotting as many differ-ent license plates as they could, or vying with each other to think of animals whose names started with each letter of the alphabet. "*Ape, bear, cheetah . . .*" Griffin hadn't thought about that trip for a long time.

He looked back at Cheyenne again. Her eyes were open but unfocused, which was kind of freaky. It reminded him of parties he had been to, people so drugged or drunk they were lost in their own world. It was weird that he could look at her and she wouldn't know.

As he watched, Cheyenne began to cough again, explosions that jerked her body around on the seat. Finally, she choked out, "Can you get me a cough drop from my purse?"

He pulled off on a gravel turnout but left the engine running. After rummaging in her purse, he found a pack of cough drops. "Here you go," he said. She opened her mouth. Even though he hadn't been to mass since his mom left when he was ten, Griffin suddenly felt like a priest with a communion wafer. As he gave Cheyenne the cough drop, his fingertips grazed her lips.

"Look," he said, "I'm going to need to cover your face for a second. And when we stop, I'll need you to stay quiet, okay?"

For a moment, the only sound was her sucking on the lozenge. Then finally she nodded.

Griffin pulled the blanket loosely over her face, then put the car in gear and drove on. As he did, he unconsciously rubbed his fingertips together, the ones that had touched her lips.

Here Be Dragons

The kidnapper couldn't see her. Nobody could see her. It was like she was invisible. As she lay on the backseat of the car, hidden under the blanket, Cheyenne allowed herself to cry without making any sound. In the last three years, she had gotten good at it.

After the accident, her dad had fallen apart. Every night in the hospital, he slept in her room. Her mom would have done the same, but her mom was gone. Her dad traveled so much on business that it was her mom who knew her best, who knew everything about her. Who else would remember that Cheyenne loved chocolate chip Teddy Grahams and was scared of moths? Who was going to take her shopping for bras and talk to her about the kids at school? In the hospital, Cheyenne's dad sometimes woke her up because he was crying in his sleep. She had realized it was her job to be strong for him, so Cheyenne had hid her real feelings, her real self, so that he wouldn't guess how bad it was.

Now, hidden under the blanket, she felt her chest ache. She didn't know how much of it was from holding the sobs in and how much was from the pneumonia. Danielle had already guessed it was pneumonia by listening with her stethoscope to the crackle in Cheyenne's lungs, as well as the dead area where there should have been breath sounds but weren't. Even though Cheyenne had never seen anything but a blurry slice of Danielle, she still had a clear mental picture of her. Blond, shoulder-length, straight hair and a slender body, looking something like one of a million actresses on TV, although Danielle was smarter than any two or three of them put together.

The visit to the doctor's office had just been a formality, a way to get the prescription that a nurse wasn't allowed to write. The doctor had tapped the X-ray, making a hollow plastic sound, and told them that it showed a shadow over the bottom of Cheyenne's right lung. "With antibiotics, we can knock this thing out in a few days. It will take you some time to regain your stamina, but you'll be well on your way to recovery by the time school starts after Christmas break."

Cheyenne took a long, shuddering breath. Her head felt like it was stuffed with cotton. Everything seemed unreal. This couldn't be happening to her. It was like those old maps from back when they thought the world was flat, where out past the land, far out in the ocean, they had written "Here be Dragons."

She took a deep breath. *Think*, Cheyenne commanded herself. *Concentrate*. She had to use whatever advantages she had. Except she didn't have any. If only Phantom were here! More than anything, she missed him. She wished she hadn't left him at home, but Danielle had thought it would be easier since all they were doing was walking from the car to the doctor's office and back, and she didn't need a guide dog for that. But if Cheyenne had had Phantom with her, this creepy guy wouldn't even have gotten in the car.

Now here she was, blind, kidnapped, tied up, and going who knows where with a criminal. Her cell phone was gone. And she was very sick.

No! Cheyenne mouthed the word to herself. She had to stay on track. Think. She was blind. That was a fact. That was her greatest weakness. But could she somehow use it to her advantage?

And there were a few advantages to being blind—not many, certainly not enough. But a few. For one thing, she knew how to use all her other senses in a way that most sighted people never did. They smelled and heard and touched all the same things she did, but they had let that part of their brain go numb with disuse, so the sensations didn't register. And Cheyenne had learned the hard way to always, always pay attention to what was around her, to pick up as many clues as she could.

So how could she use her senses to her advantage? She sniffed, but all she could smell was the stale residue of the cigarette smoke on this guy's clothes. Until they stopped and he opened the door, she wouldn't have any clues from her nose. Her ears told her just as little. All she knew was that it had been at least twenty minutes since another car had passed them. And she had long ago lost track of the direction they were headed. They had been on a winding road for a while—but for how long? She twisted her hands until she could run her thumb over the numbers on her Braille watch. It was almost eleven. This guy had stolen the car about forty-five minutes ago. Okay, so they were forty-five miles or less away from the mall. She roughed out the math problem in her head. The result was disheartening. That meant she could be anywhere within a space a little greater than six thousand square miles. Even if they stopped soon, how could her dad and Danielle or even the police find her in all that space?

Cheyenne forced her mind back to the things she might be able to control. Like the guy who had kidnapped her. What could she do to get an advantage over him?

She decided that the first step would be to get him to untie her. Poor blindy, that's what she had to make him think. Once she could use her hands, she could find a phone. Or a weapon. She could even take her cane and run away as soon as it was dark. She longed for it to be nighttime, when she would be more than a sighted person's equal.

When they got wherever they were going, she would talk him into freeing her hands. Then she would collect all the clues and tools she could and bide her time. And if it seemed like he was going to do something bad, she wouldn't go quietly. She would give him the fight of his life.

It seemed impossible, but Cheyenne must have fallen asleep. The next thing she knew, the car was lurching down a gravel road so bumpy she almost rolled off the seat. Over the noise in the cab, she heard a dog barking. Judging by how deep the sound was, it was a big dog. And not very well trained.

Another noise was layered over the barking, a high-pitched metallic whine. A saw. The sound, which was coming from someplace in front of the car, abruptly ceased. The window whirred as it glided down. Cold seeped in and pressed against her, even under the blanket. The smells of wood smoke and pine needles filled the car.

The dog stopped barking and started to whine. Footsteps crunched on gravel. Cheyenne's problem had just gotten twice as complicated. Now there were two people, not one. But maybe this new person would see how ridiculous it was that she was a prisoner. Maybe he or she—it would be a lot better if it were a she—would insist that Cheyenne be freed immediately.

But it was a man who spoke, in a rough voice that

mingled interest and suspicion. "God damn, Griffin, what's this?" Cheyenne filed the name away. *Griffin.* If she ever got free—she quickly amended that to *when*—she would make this Griffin pay. "Where'd you get it?"

"At the mall. Somebody left the keys in it."

"God damn!" The same words, only this time filled with respect. "But what happened to your face?" Good, she *had* hurt Griffin. Then the other man must have realized what was under the blanket, because his tone changed. "What in hell is that in the backseat?"

"It's a girl."

"You killed a girl!" Disbelief.

"No, no," Griffin said hastily. "She's just tied up. She was in the car. Lying down in the backseat. I didn't see her at first. And by the time I did, it was too late. So I had to take her with me."

The smack of flesh meeting flesh. Cheyenne realized that the other man had just slapped Griffin.

"So you brought her back here? That wasn't a real smart idea. Why am I not surprised that it was you that thought of it?"

"What else did you want me to do?" Griffin whined. "In five more minutes, the place would have been crawling with cops. I had to get away as fast as I could. I'll just wait until tonight, and go drop her out on a logging road. And then I'll hightail it out of there."

"You idiot! She knows what you look like. And now

she's been here. I don't need to spell it out for you. She'll say who we are. She'll get the cops back here. Are you trying to back me into a corner?"

"But she's blind, Dad!"

Dad?

In Case the Law Comes Looking

"Give me her purse," Roy demanded. He held out his hand. "Let's see who she is." He was still angry, that was clear, but Roy was always at least a little bit angry.

The thing was, Griffin thought, watching his dad carefully, his cheek still stinging, how angry was he?

"I already know who she is. Her name's Cheyenne Wilder."

He got out of the car. Roy took a step closer. He was all up in Griffin's face now, nose to nose, which was kind of a surprise. How long had he been nose to nose, eye to eye, with his dad? Sensing the tension, Duke started growling.

Griffin stepped back, holding his hands up in surrender.

His dad spit tobacco out of the side of his mouth. Roy was nothing but muscle and tattoo. Despite the cold, Roy was dressed the way he always was, in a black leather

Harley vest open over a flannel shirt. The sleeves of the shirt had been torn off, ragged over his bulging pecs. The Skoal can in his chest pocket had left a faded circle on the plaid.

Jimbo and TJ came out of the barn. Griffin was glad for the distraction.

"Whoa! What is that?" Jimbo asked, shaking his head in admiration as he took in the Escalade. Even though he had plenty of personal insulation, Jimbo was wearing so many layers he looked like the Michelin man. Jimbo was always cold. "A little something you picked up shopping?"

"Sweet!" TJ chimed in. TJ was skinny and short, not much taller than Cheyenne, with a long dirty blond ponytail poking out of the back of his trucker's cap.

"Only there's a problem," Roy said. The red in his face had faded slightly. "The car came with a little something extra. A girl."

"A kid," Griffin felt the need to interject. He could already see TJ perking up, and he didn't need him to get the wrong idea. "And actually, she's blind, so she didn't see anything."

The two men peered through the half-open window at Cheyenne. Underneath the blanket, she was absolutely still. Griffin hoped she couldn't hear exactly what they were saying.

"So she's really blind?" TJ asked in a loud voice.

Griffin saw her flinch under the blanket.

Jimbo nudged TJ. "He said blind, dummy, not deaf."

Roy turned his head to spit tobacco juice. "Did you change the plates?"

"Hey, I didn't know I was going to find a car. I didn't bring any with me."

"Where's the Honda?"

Griffin didn't want to answer, but he had to. "I had to leave it there."

"Where's it at? Don't tell me it's anywhere near where you got this."

"The Honda is in the far end, by Borders," Griffin said. "And the Escalade was on the complete opposite end of the parking lot."

"We can't leave it there overnight or someone might connect the dots between one car left in the parking lot and another car that got stolen." Roy thought for a moment. "Give them the keys. You two can take the pickup and go out to Woodlands and get the Honda back."

TJ and Jimbo mumbled agreement. Griffin tossed Jimbo the keys and the two men ambled off toward the pickup. When they were out of earshot, Roy turned to him.

"You've got us in a world of hurt, you know that? For right now, get her in the house. Keep her hands tied up, put her some place she can't cause any problems, and then come back here. I'll put the Escalade in the barn. Don't use names and don't tell her where we are. You and me need to talk about what we're going to do. But not in front of her."

When Griffin opened the car door and leaned in,

Cheyenne's body was rigid. As he pulled the blanket back, she rubbed her cheek on the striped scarf she wore around her neck, over her coat. She was, he realized, wiping away tears. The dampness still shone on her red face. It seemed strange that she could cry even when her eyes didn't otherwise work.

He helped her sit up and then said, "I'm going to cut the shoelaces around your ankles now. Don't move." He took out his knife, unfolded the blade. So that he wouldn't slip and cut her, he put one hand between her ankles, just below the taut shoelace, and felt how she trembled.

After cutting the shoelace loose, Griffin helped her up into a sitting position. As he did, Cheyenne whispered to him.

"Just give me my cane and let me go right now. I won't tell anyone anything. I promise."

He kept his answer short. "No." He concentrated on slipping on her laceless shoes.

"Then tonight, when everyone's asleep."

He shook his head and then realized she couldn't see him. But she must have felt the movement because she pressed her lips together until they were a thin white line.

Leaving her purse and her cane on the floor, Griffin began to help Cheyenne out of the car. Duke, not used to seeing strangers, exploded in a frenzy of barking. He strained against the length of his chain.

Instead of shrinking back against Griffin, the way any

normal person would, or provoking Duke by trying to run away, Cheyenne stopped and was absolutely still, her head cocked.

The dog didn't seem to know what to think. Griffin doubted he had ever met a human who didn't regard him with fear or kick him with a steel-toed boot. He stopped barking and eyed Cheyenne, a low growl still rumbling in his throat. Roy was staring at Duke, looking back and forth between the dog and Cheyenne. It was the first time Griffin could remember Duke shutting up in the presence of a stranger.

Basically, Duke didn't like new things. If a car came down the road, they knew it long before it showed up. And nobody could just walk around their property, not without Duke throwing himself to the end of his chain, barking and growling. The dog allowed only Roy or Griffin to feed him, and he barely tolerated that. Anyone else who came too near risked losing a body part.

Roy hadn't bought Duke or gotten him at the pound. Duke had been given to him by a customer who sold a little of this and a little of that. The guy had had a big bloody bandage around his upper arm and he had kept his distance from Duke, not really relaxing until he was back behind the wheel of his truck, with a metal door between him and the dog.

Duke was just the kind of dog Griffin's dad had been looking for.

"Easy, boy," Griffin said now into the silence, pretending like Duke was acting normally. "She's with us." Then he nudged the girl forward. "We need to get you in the house."

They started walking. Griffin kept his hand on her arm. "What kind of dog is he?" Cheyenne said as calmly as if they were talking about somebody's pet.

"Him? Half pit bull and half mystery meat."

All muscle and no heart. In truth, Griffin didn't know what kind of dog Duke was. He looked like he had been put together from a half dozen different dogs, taking only the ugliest parts. He had the short, sleek fur of a pit bull, brindled brown and gold, but scars from fighting marred the tiger's-eye pattern. One ear stood up, and the other flopped down. His legs were a little too short, and his tail was all wrong for a junkyard dog—fluffy and curved. And with his one droopy eyelid, Duke looked sly. Like he was plotting something.

Now, as they walked toward the house, Griffin found himself strangely glad that Cheyenne couldn't see where he lived. Just having her by his side made him view the whole place the way a stranger might. It had been a long time since a stranger was out here. Roy didn't like strangers much.

They were set well back from the road. At the end of the driveway, where Griffin had left the Escalade, was the barn. One of the barn doors stood open. Inside were compressors, welding equipment, an engine lift, and a beat-up flatbed truck. The barn was where they did most of their work, but the overflow spilled out onto the lawn. Only it wasn't really a lawn, just bare patches alternating with weeds. A bumper lay here; a car door, there. Back by the fence, a minivan, stripped of its wheels, looked more like a crushed shoe box.

A long time ago, back when Griffin's dad had had a job, on weekends he also worked as a shade tree mechanic, among other things. Then he got fired and one thing led to another, to the point where TJ and Jimbo were employees, if you could call them that. A chop shop sounded kind of organized, like an assembly line of thieves. They were anything but. Take a bunch of guys with no women around, throw in cars and car parts and machinery and tools, and you had the recipe for a real mess.

People out in these parts didn't think twice about leaving a rusting pickup up on blocks in the driveway or hauling an old washing machine out to the long grass. Griffin and Roy's place just looked a little worse than most. But in case the law came looking, most of the operation was out of sight, out of mind. The barn hid their activities from prying eyes, even from the air. And once a vehicle had been stripped of all usable parts, TJ or Jimbo would eventually get out the Cat and bury the skeleton out back.

West of the barn was the house. It was a few decades newer than the barn, but it had needed painting ever since Griffin could remember. Now the paint curled up in long, rusty red strips.

Behind the house rose forested hills where nobody noticed if you shot a deer—in season or not. A few hardwoods were sprinkled among the evergreens, brilliant orange and red in the fall but bare and gaunt now. But mostly the forest was rich green pine and Douglas fir. Somebody owned the land, the government or maybe some rich guy back East. Griffin had heard it both ways. But whoever owned it never came around, so Griffin thought of it as his own personal forest.

Cheyenne caught her toe on a crankshaft and stumbled into Griffin. "Sorry, sorry," he mumbled. It was hard to look ahead and think what might trip her up. Feeling contrite, he steered her around broken gears, a windshield wiper, and a gas cap.

They reached the front steps. At the last minute, he remembered to say, "Step up."

Turning Secrets into Weapons

The house smelled funky, like mold, bacon grease, and cigarettes. The floors were bare. Cheyenne could tell by the sound of their footsteps that they were made of wood, not tile or linoleum. She shuffled her feet so that she could hear the echo from the walls. The rooms sounded small.

She wished her hands were free so she could protect her belly. She kept hitting her shins, knees, and stomach on furniture and other unknown obstacles. Sometimes she could sense things ahead of her, but the way Griffin was hustling her forward, she didn't have time. Her body was already mapping this house in bruises. If only Phantom were here. Griffin was terrible at guiding her.

Griffin. She held the name close to her, like a gift. His name was Griffin. There was a kid at her high school named that, a senior. But the name wasn't that common. Once she got free—and she would get free, she had to—his name might be just the clue the police needed to find them and lock them all up.

Then Griffin would be the one stumbling with his hands bound behind him.

And there was Griffin's dad. What kind of a dad thought it was okay for his kid to be out stealing cars? Cheyenne thought she had heard one of the two other men say his name before they left. Ray? No, Roy, that was it. At least she thought so.

Cheyenne resolved to keep whatever secrets she could. Maybe, just maybe, she could turn them into weapons. Take her blindness, for example. A lot of blind people weren't totally blind. Including Cheyenne. Cheyenne could see a little out of her left eye, but Griffin didn't know that.

The doctors had called what had happened to her a contracoup injury. The blow had hit her forehead, but the damage had happened when her brain bounced off the back of her skull.

Even three years later, Cheyenne still remembered snippets of what the doctors had said standing over her hospital bed. Her dad had sat by her and cried. Cheyenne had had a tube down her throat, so she couldn't talk. There were more tubes in her nose and arms. She had kept her eyes closed and pretended to be asleep while they explained what the injuries were and what they meant.

"Occipital lobe injury." "Damage to the visual cortex." "Wiped out the vascular system in the back of the brain."

What it meant was that all of Cheyenne's central vision—the 20/20 part, what most people thought of as seeing—was gone. Most of her peripheral vision was gone, too. She had been left with only one ten-degree slice on the very left edge of what had been her old field of vision. But the problem with peripheral vision was that it wasn't 20/20, but 20/200. Legally blind. The way the edges of everyone's vision were, except they didn't know it. People saw with clarity only whatever they focused on, not what lay on the sides. So now what a normal person could see at two hundred feet, Cheyenne could see a tiny slice of at twenty feet.

What she was left with was a blurred sliver of color and shapes that usually was more distracting than helpful. Now, if she wanted to see anything at all, she had to turn her head away from it. It seemed like a metaphor, but Cheyenne didn't know for what.

Paying attention to that slice of vision usually only gave Cheyenne a headache and didn't yield anything useful. A lot of times she just closed her eyes or wore dark glasses. For one thing, it made other people feel more comfortable. They didn't like to talk to someone who might or might not be looking directly at their eyes.

The sound of her footsteps changed. The space had narrowed even further. A hall. It was colder here. She felt Griffin lean past her. A door creaked open. He nudged her forward. Once they were inside, Griffin put his hands on her shoulders and turned her around to face him.

"Sit down. There's a bed just behind you."

A bed. The thought made her nervous. Maybe it made Griffin nervous, too, because his voice was too loud, the way sighted people often were when they talked to her.

"Can you untie my hands?" She stood with her shoulders curled over and made her voice weak and small. She wanted Griffin to see her like that.

Cheyenne tried not to think about how she really was weak and small.

"No," he said in a tone that said there was no use arguing. "Now, sit down on the bed."

Cheyenne shuffled backward until she could feel the mattress against the backs of her knees. She sat. She heard him run out of the room, but before she could react, he was back. Until she felt him touch her ankle, she didn't know Griffin had crouched down next to her. She let out a little shriek that immediately shamed her.

"Sorry," he said. "I just have to tie you to the bed so you don't take off." She felt a smooth narrow cord go around one ankle. "I'll leave you enough slack so that you can lie down." His hands finished the knot and then tugged at it. "Okay. Now you're going to have to stay in here for a while. Don't even think of trying to get away. We're miles from nowhere. And even if you did manage to get out into the yard, Duke would swallow you whole for supper."

Duke, Cheyenne thought. Griffin and Duke and Roy. And doing something with electric saws out in the middle of nowhere. There can only be one place like this.

"Please, mister," she said, "can I have a glass of water?" There. Maybe calling Griffin "mister" would make him think she didn't know his name. Cheyenne gave a little fake cough, but it quickly turned into a real one. She coughed and coughed until her lungs ached. She heard him leave again, then water running, his footsteps hurrying back.

"Here." He put his hand on the back of her head and tried to tilt the glass to her lips. Most of it sloshed over her coat. Some of it ran down her neck. Cheyenne gulped, choked, sputtered. A little of it went down her throat, which felt as if it were on fire. Awkwardly, he patted her face with her scarf.

"You should lie down," he finally said. She heard him set the glass down. "I'll be back later."

He closed the door. She listened for the sound of his footsteps disappearing down the hall. The front door opened and closed. As soon as it did, she rolled off the bed and began to search. With her leg tethered, she was only able to get a few feet from the bed. But Cheyenne used her free foot. She turned around and fluttered her fingers against anything she could reach with her hands tied behind her back, even bent forward from the waist and literally nosed around what she thought was a desk.

She didn't know what she was searching for, and she didn't know that she would know even if she found it. Cheyenne needed something. Something that would tip the balance. She knew it was too much to hope for a pocket-knife, a telephone, a pair of scissors. But even a pen would be good. She might be able to hide a pen and use it later to stab someone. The room was surprisingly neat and empty. Even though they didn't seem like the kind of people who would have a guest room, maybe that's what this was.

The only useful item Cheyenne found was on top of the desk. She ran into it with her nose and nearly tipped it on its side. The glass! She hooked it with her chin and pulled it back to the edge of the desk. Then she turned around and grabbed it with the fingers of her bound hands.

Whole it was nothing. But broken? She pinched the top edge between the thumb and fingers of her right hand. Without giving herself time to think, she swung her hand in a short, sharp arc that ended when the glass hit the edge of the dresser.

This Might Change Things

Walking back to the barn, Griffin thought that he had never had a girl in his room before, let alone on his bed.

And it was weird to be able to look right at someone and know that they had no idea that you were looking at them. And you could stare as long as you wanted without ever worrying about being caught. Although if Cheyenne hadn't told him she was blind, Griffin might not have known. When he spoke, she seemed to look right at him. Maybe her right eye wandered a bit, that was all. She had beautiful eyes, so dark they looked all pupil.

It was easier to think about her being blind than it was about what to do now. Griffin wished life was like one of the computers at his old school, that he could just make a few clicks and restore things to the way they had been five minutes before he spotted the keys dangling from the Escalade's ignition. Instead, he had made one impulsive decision after another, and now he was stuck with the results.

Griffin lit the cigarette Cheyenne had made him take out of his mouth earlier. He could hear the radio playing from inside the barn. The sound floated on the crisp air. For some reason, TJ and Jimbo liked to listen to this right-wing radio talk-show host, some guy who was constantly going off about illegals and HMOs and homos. Griffin thought it was kind of funny how they were always agreeing with him, saying "damn straight!" when the radio host would probably have happily strung up the two of them himself.

Iced-over puddles cracked under his feet. It hadn't snowed yet, but it felt like it might. Griffin liked how the snow shook a white blanket over everything, softening all the edges. Take the remains of one car—a Honda that had been relieved of its wheels, door panels, seats, and stereo—sitting midway between the house and the barn. Covered in snow, it would become a beautiful, abstract sculpture.

His dad had driven the Escalade into the barn and was now walking around it, eyeing it up and down. The SUV was cherry. It had less than fifteen thousand miles on it. Stealing it should have been a real coup. It would have shown his dad that Griffin was capable of playing in the big leagues—if Cheyenne hadn't been in the back. But that was a pretty big if.

"Are you going to replace the VINs?" Griffin asked Roy. A VIN—vehicle identification number—was stamped in several places on all cars. Basically, it was a car's fingerprint. But you could take the VIN from a salvaged car and put it onto a stolen car, in essence swapping the fingerprint of a wanted car for a legal one.

Roy ran his thumb over his lip. "I don't know. It's probably too hot to risk it. I'm thinking maybe we should just slap some new plates on it for a bit and have you ditch it up in Washington, like the forest or something. You could throw that old moped in the back, and then when you got there put the old plates back on and wipe the whole thing down and use the moped to get back. Leave it someplace it won't get found until next spring."

"We could get fifteen grand for it, easy," Griffin protested.

"We could get fifteen *years* for it, easy." There was an edge to Roy's voice. "In Oregon, there's minimum sentences for kidnapping and no plea-bargaining. If anyone finds out we're involved, we'll be in deep for sure." The anger returned, as Griffin had known it would. "Just what in the hell do you think you're going to do with her?"

They had been living on the wrong side of the law for a long time, but it had always been property crimes. Folks who lived around here maybe knew that Roy ran an odd little body shop. But they weren't the kind to ask questions about why it didn't advertise in the yellow pages, didn't have a sign out front, and didn't accept customers off the street.

"Look, she can't even see us," Griffin said. "So she can't say what we look like. She doesn't know our names. She has no idea where we are. We can keep the car and trade plates and VINs. And tonight I'll drive her out to the middle of nowhere and make her get out. By the time anybody finds her, I'll be long gone."

But Roy had stopped paying attention to Griffin. He was holding up one hand, his eyes narrowed down to slits as he listened to the radio.

The announcer was saying, "Coming up in the noon news—police are investigating the daring kidnapping of the sixteen-year-old daughter of Nike's president. She was taken at ten this morning from the Woodlands Experience shopping center."

Nike's president? Griffin thought. Nike had started out as a running shoe company but now made clothes and shoes for every kind of sport or for people who just liked the look of their clothes.

Roy turned up the radio. In silence, the two of them listened to two commercials, one for a law firm, the other for Burgerville.

The female announcer came back. She said breathlessly, "Police say sixteen-year-old Cheyenne Wilder, daughter of Nike's president, Nick Wilder, was kidnapped shortly after ten this morning at the Woodlands Experience shopping center. Her father spoke to reporters a few minutes ago."

A man's voice, strained but professional sounding, said, "My daughter is blind. We lost her mother three years ago in the same accident that took Cheyenne's sight. And

Cheyenne's also very ill. In fact, she was returning from the doctor's office when she was kidnapped. If she doesn't receive treatment immediately, she could die."

The announcer cut in. "Police say Cheyenne and her stepmother stopped at the pharmacy to pick up a prescription. The stepmother, Danielle Wilder, went in alone to get it, and that's when the girl was taken. She is described as five foot two, one hundred five pounds, with brown eyes and long, dark, curly hair. She was last seen wearing a black tracksuit and a silver down coat. The car is a dark green Cadillac Escalade SUV, license number 396CVS. While there are reports of the car being driven at a high rate of speed out of the parking lot, witnesses were unable to give a good description of the person driving the car. An AMBER Alert has been issued. If you spot the vehicle, police ask that you call 9-1-1." The announcer took a breath. "In other news . . ." Roy turned down the radio.

Griffin braced himself for the outburst he knew would come. The car was not just hot, it was on fire. And the girl was more a problem than ever.

But Roy just looked thoughtful. He turned, spit a stream of tobacco juice, and wiped the back of his mouth with his hand.

"President of Nike, huh?" Roy looked toward the house. "We need to think about this a little more. This might change things."

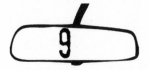

Stealing a Girl

The glass bounced off the edge of the dresser. It quivered in Cheyenne's fingers but didn't break. With her hands tied, it was hard to put much strength behind what was basically just a flick of her wrist. And a little part of her was afraid of cutting herself.

Cheyenne steeled herself and swung harder.

With a ringing sound, the glass bounced off again, unscathed.

She reminded herself that she had more to fear than getting cut. What these men might do to her was much, much worse. When next Cheyenne swung the glass, she pivoted with her hips and twisted her wrist as hard as she could.

Time seemed to slow down. She felt the impact and then the cracks radiating out as the glass split and broke. Cheyenne was left holding one large piece while several others pinged off the floor. Gingerly, she strained with the fingers of her free hand to explore the piece she still held. It was about two inches long and an inch wide. The edges were curved and very sharp. Even touching them lightly, she was afraid. It was like running her fingertip along a knife's edge, full of dangerous promise. Her heart was beating in her ears.

What should she do first? The cord that tied her to the bed would be easier to cut, but she would still have her hands bound behind her. Cheyenne decided to concentrate on cutting the shoestring around her wrists.

She gritted her teeth and twisted her hand until the edge of the glass rested on the shoelace. The position was almost impossible to maintain. The tension ran all the way up to her shoulder blades. Then she realized she needed to turn her hand even farther, or she would risk slicing her left wrist as well as the shoestring. She gritted her teeth, twisted her wrist, and began to saw.

In her mind's eye, the shoestring was white. She had never asked anyone what color her shoestrings were, but white was the only color that made sense. Cheyenne knew that her shoes were light blue and that—before the accident at least—shoelaces had pretty much come in white, brown, or black. So it was probably white, and that was how she pictured it. Cheyenne still "saw" things, even things she had never laid eyes on before the accident. And it was more than just the little blurry slice of vision she had left.

She didn't know what it was like for those who had been born blind, but for her, imagining that she could still see, as if she had simply closed her eyes and could open them to view the world at any time, helped her to create mental maps of rooms and buildings and even neighborhoods. And the maps made it easier for her to move around, whether it was in her room at home (where she really had seen most things before she lost her sight), or at her school or through downtown Portland (both places where her mental maps had to be built from a combination of imagination and memory).

So in Cheyenne's mind, the shoelace was white, the bedpost she was tied to was painted brown, and the soft quilt on the bed was made up of alternating squares of white and pale yellow. And even if she twisted her head and concentrated, her sliver of vision might not be clear enough to confirm any of this.

The doctors said it was good practice to hold on to her visual memory and to exercise her skills as long as she could. Because she had been born sighted, Cheyenne still related to the world the way a sighted person would. When she dreamed, she still saw colors and faces, furniture and flowers, and was shocked when she woke up and realized she couldn't see any of those things. And deep inside herself, Cheyenne cherished the hope that someday she would see again. Every few months, her dad would read her some story in the paper about experiments with computers or implants. Danielle didn't like that he read these stories to Cheyenne. She talked about raising false hope. But Cheyenne had long ago decided that she would rather have false hope than no hope at all.

Sure, Cheyenne had learned how to "travel" with a cane—which was what the professional blind people called it. She had learned to use a computer that spoke to her. She had learned how to organize her clothes so they weren't inside out or clashing. She could cook, eat, put on makeup, do her nails, fix her hair. But it still couldn't take away the times when she said something about a person she thought wasn't in the room—only they were. Or the cashiers who saw Cheyenne put the clothes on the counter and open her wallet and still said to her friends Kenzie or Sadie, "Will she be paying by check or credit card?" As if she wasn't capable of speech.

The room was cold, but Cheyenne's hands were sweating, making it hard to keep a good hold on the broken piece of glass. The tendons in her wrist ached. She ignored everything but the thought that soon she would have her hands free.

A noise made her freeze. It sounded like a door swinging open at the far end of the house. Cheyenne recognized Griffin's voice, and that of his dad. She had a few seconds, maybe less. With the side of her free foot, she tried to sweep the other shards of glass under the dresser. Straining her wrist until it felt like it might snap, she managed to slip the broken piece of glass into her coat pocket. By the time she heard the doorknob turn, Cheyenne was again sitting on the bed, sweat running cold down her back. In her mind's eye, she imagined several pieces of glass still lying in the middle of the floor. Winking in the light. Giving her away. Taking a deep, shuddering breath, she told herself there was nothing she could do about it now.

The door swung open. Their first words were a surprise.

"Why didn't you tell me who you were?" demanded Griffin.

Cheyenne felt confused. Now that she was no longer concentrating so fiercely on cutting away her bonds, exhaustion and sickness crashed over her like a wave. "I did tell you. I'm Cheyenne Wilder."

Roy said, "But you're the daughter of Nike's president."

"How do you know that?" She spent most of her time trying to play it down. Even at the private school that she attended, where everyone's parents were doctors or lawyers, people acted like what her dad did was a big deal. All it meant was that he traveled a lot and that the whole family dressed in Nike—and Harley, Converse, and Cole Haan—clothes from head to toe. And sometimes she met famous athletes.

"There was a story about you on the radio," Griffin said. "Your dad said you were so sick that you could die. I just thought you had a cold or something."

Her dad! Cheyenne's chest ached so bad. She didn't

know if it was from the pneumonia or because she needed to cry. She wished she could hear her dad's voice. To hear one good thing on this awful day.

Roy stepped closer. He smelled gross. She sniffed again. Peppermint chewing tobacco, like one of the kids on the football team chewed, the sharp smell of mint not masking the earthy, stomach-turning smell of tobacco. "So how sick are you?"

Cheyenne was strangely torn. She wanted to act like everything was okay, to not show any weakness. But then she remembered what she had thought earlier when she was alone with Griffin. It was probably better to let them know that she was sick. Because maybe they would watch her less closely, leave her alone more. They would think she was too weak to pose any danger.

"I've got pneumonia. That's why we were at the pharmacy—to get my antibiotic prescription filled."

"And your mom left you in the car," Griffin said.

Cheyenne shook her head. Suddenly, the distinction seemed important. "Danielle's my stepmom. My real mom's dead. Danielle left the keys in the car in case I got cold." She remembered how she had begged Danielle to leave the keys and pushed the thought away.

"Well, now we need her number and everyone else's," Roy demanded. "Cell phone numbers for your dad and stepmom, home number, work numbers. And we also need to know how much you think your daddy might part with."

He paused to let that sink in. "Here's a tip. It had better be a lot."

Cheyenne had thought that Griffin had only been stealing a car. But now it looked like he had been stealing a girl, too.

The Etiquette of Kidnapping

Cheyenne looked frightened. "Most of my phone numbers are programmed into my cell phone." Her voice was ragged. "It's voice activated. I just say who I want to call, and it dials it for me."

"So it's in the car?" Roy turned toward the door.

"I threw it out the window." Griffin hoped Roy wasn't going to get mad. It wasn't always easy to know what would set his dad off. "It started ringing, and I was worried they could trace it. So I threw it in some bushes in a vacant lot near the shopping center."

"Good point," Roy said, nodding. Then he turned to Cheyenne. "Just tell me all the numbers you remember."

"My home number is five oh three—"

"Hold on, hold on," Roy said. Griffin saw that his dad didn't have a piece of paper or anything to write with. Roy went out and began scrabbling in the junk drawer in the kitchen, leaving Griffin alone with Cheyenne.

She didn't look good, in Griffin's opinion. Her cheeks were red, but the rest of her face was blue-white, like skim milk. And then she started coughing again. Thick, wet coughs that sounded like something was tearing in her chest. The cords stood out in her neck. Griffin turned to get her some more water, but the glass wasn't on the dresser where he thought he had left it. He went into the kitchen to get another one, leaving the room just as Roy came in with a pencil stub and a piece of torn paper.

The kitchen looked the way it always did, but imagining what Cheyenne would think if she could see it made Griffin look at it differently. Dirty dishes were piled in the sink. On the stove, every burner held a pan with the remains of some kind of food stuck to the bottom. The counter was crowded with empty cans, open cereal boxes, tipped-over beer bottles, and overflowing ashtrays. The only time anything got washed was if Griffin grew too disgusted to let it go on any longer. The problem with him being the one who occasionally cleaned up was that Roy expected it.

There weren't any clean glasses in the cupboard, so Griffin picked up one that didn't look too dirty and rinsed it out before filling it with cold water. When he carried it back, Cheyenne was managing to choke out numbers that his dad was writing down. He waited for them to finish. After he had written the last number down, Roy walked out of the room and motioned for Griffin to follow.

In the hall, Roy said in a low voice, "You'll need to stay here and watch her. I'm going to go make a deal for a cell phone that can't be traced. And then I'll make some calls."

"Can't I go with you?"

"Somebody needs to stay with her." Roy jerked his chin in Cheyenne's direction. She seemed to be staring at them. Griffin wondered how much she could hear. Weren't your other senses supposed to get better when you were blind?

Roy walked back down the hall, and Griffin returned to his room. "I brought you more water."

She didn't answer him for a second. He heard the front door close and realized she had been waiting until they were alone.

"You're going to have to untie my hands so I can drink it myself." It was eerie how her dark eyes seemed to be staring at him. "Last time I almost drowned."

He wondered if it was a trick. But her ankle was tied to the bed. And she wouldn't be able to move more than a few feet in an unfamiliar house before he could tackle her. Then he remembered how she had fought him in the car.

"All right. But remember, I still have a gun. If you try anything, I'll shoot you." The words were such a cliché that he worried he would laugh when he said them out loud. But instead, he sounded tough. He sounded real. He sounded scary.

He kind of liked it.

Griffin got out his penknife—his fingers brushing the knob of the cigarette lighter—and cut the shoelace around

Cheyenne's wrists. She must have been twisting her hands, because it felt frayed. She spent a few moments rubbing her wrists. At first he thought she was exaggerating but then he saw the red lines braceleting them.

Griffin put the glass in her hands. She drank without stopping and held it back out. "Can I have some more, please?"

He thought about saying no, then changed his mind. Instead, when he went out to the kitchen, he left the water running in the sink. Then he darted back on tiptoe to watch her. He had thought he would probably find her trying to untie her ankle, but instead she was still rubbing her wrists. Her expression looked beaten down, and unexpectedly he found himself disappointed. Griffin went back into the kitchen and finished refilling the glass.

While she was drinking it, his stomach growled loud enough that she turned her head in his direction. He looked at the clock by the bed. It was nearly one o'clock. "I'm going to make some lunch. Are you hungry?" The oddness of the question struck him. What was the etiquette for how to treat someone you had kidnapped?

Cheyenne shrugged. "I guess."

Back in the kitchen, he looked through the fridge. There was a package of hot dogs that hadn't been opened. No buns in the cupboard, but they had bread.

Every few minutes he tiptoed back to look at Cheyenne, but each time she hadn't moved.

Hope and Fear

Cheyenne put the can of Coke between her knees so she would know where it was. It was better than having to find it by running her hand over the table until she bumped it with the back of her fingers. After Griffin had untied her ankle, he had led her here, to what she assumed was the dining room, and then retied her ankle to a rung of the chair she now sat in. Given enough time, Cheyenne was sure she could untie herself. But when would she be given enough time?

Before they had been able to sit down at the table, Griffin had had to shove a lot of stuff aside, confirming what Cheyenne had already begun to believe about the house. People might live here, but this was a house, not a home. Nobody cared about it. Except for the room where Griffin had first taken her, everything seemed messy. Whenever he led her around, he had to jerk her to one side or the other, or he kicked things out of the way, swearing under his breath.

In her right hand, she held a hot dog wrapped in a piece of bread. The hot dog had been boiled until the skin split. The bread hadn't even been toasted. It didn't matter much because she wasn't hungry. And it was easier to eat than something that required a knife and fork. No scraping her utensils across her plate, trying to figure out where the food was. She never liked eating with anyone besides Dad and Danielle. What if she splashed sauce on her top or she was grinning away with something green wrapped around a tooth?

"When you eat, how do you know where the food is?" Griffin asked.

"My dad likes to tell me like he's a fighter pilot. You know"—she deepened her voice—"the peas are at eleven o'clock, the meat loaf is at two, and you've got mashed potatoes coming in at seven o'clock."

Griffin laughed. For a second, Cheyenne forgot she wasn't talking to a friend, like Sadie or Kenzie. But only for a second.

She spoke around another bite of hot dog. "He used to cut up my food for me, because he was afraid I would choke. It was really embarrassing, especially if we were in public." Secretly, Cheyenne always hoped people still took her for a sighted person. In restaurants or movie theaters, she would try to tuck her cane out of sight. Everyone told

Cheyenne that she didn't look blind, that she looked "normal." If she hid her cane, then people talked to her, not to whoever was with her. Everything changed if they figured out she was blind. She was tired of waiters who took everyone else's order and then said, "And what will she be having?"

Griffin said, "Even if someone tells you where everything is, it must be hard to find it on your plate."

"That's why I bring my lunch to school. Then I can just unwrap and eat one thing at a time. And since I made it, I know exactly what it is."

Another reason Cheyenne brought her own lunch was that she didn't want anyone to have to carry her tray for her. People had to help her enough already, without her asking for more. She didn't like to accept more than she could give back. She kept a mental tally of people who did favors for her, and she tried to keep the balance sheet even. If she helped Kenzie with an essay for English, then it was okay for Cheyenne to accept Kenzie's offer of a ride home.

"You know what?" Griffin asked. "The whole time you've been talking, I've been trying to eat with my eyes closed. It's harder than you would think."

Cheyenne resisted saying something sarcastic. Sometimes people did this, closed their eyes for a few seconds and imagined it gave them insights into what it was like to be her. Only, at the end, they could still open their eyes and see.

Instead she said, "You know what I miss? Like if you have a baked potato and it has some cheese on top but it all ended up melted on one spot? When I could see, I could move the cheese around so I got some in every bite. Or if there was something I didn't like in a casserole, like green peppers, I could pick them out. Now I usually just eat whatever ends up on my fork, even if I don't like it very much."

Every word Cheyenne was saying was true, but it was also a mask, a lie to lull Griffin into relaxing around her. She had heard Roy's car start up and drive off. Since then, there had been quiet. No vehicle engines, no whining saws. Even the dog was no longer barking.

Cheyenne thought it was just her and Griffin. In the house, for sure. Maybe, if she was lucky, the rest of them were gone from the property, too. However many there were. She had heard four voices while she was in the car, too terrified to move—Griffin, his dad, and two other men. Of course, it was possible there were even more but they just hadn't spoken. She hoped the vehicle that had been driven away as they were walking into the house meant the other two men had left, too.

So she was pretty sure she and Griffin were alone. But how long would it be before one of the other three men came back? This might be her only chance.

She popped the last bite of hot dog into her mouth. Trying to sound casual, she shifted the food into her cheek and mumbled, "I have to go to the bathroom."

"All right. Just a second. I have to untie you."

He knelt beside her. For a second, Cheyenne wondered if there was a knife on the table. Did she have the strength— emotional and physical—to bury it between his shoulder blades? Could she kill a person if her own life was on the line? And was her life on the line? Maybe these men would ask for ransom and then let her go. But wasn't it just as likely that they would take the money and never give her back?

Griffin finished untying her ankle, then helped her to her feet and led her down the hall. He opened a door. "The sink's to your right, the tub's on your left, and the toilet is all the way back on your right."

"I'm going to turn the water on in the sink a little bit," Cheyenne said. "Just for some privacy." She emphasized the word *privacy*. Hoping to embarrass him a little. Hoping to push him farther away from the door.

As Griffin closed the door behind Cheyenne, she put her hand on her side of the knob. Her fingers pushed in the lock button just as it closed. If Griffin heard it, he would think she just wanted to be sure she was alone, and she did. But not for what he was thinking. Even the lock wouldn't buy her much time. No more than a minute or two. But maybe a minute would be enough.

Then Cheyenne walked straight back, hands outstretched, kicking her feet a little ahead of her so she wouldn't stumble over a dirty towel or the sink pedestal. On her left, her fingers brushed a plastic shower curtain. When she found the sink, she paused for a second to turn on the water. Not full blast, but enough to hide small noises.

Griffin hadn't said anything about a window, but even before she reached it she could feel the air change. When she touched it, the pane was cold. She could tell it was made of those honeycomb panels that blurred but did not entirely hide what was behind them. Was someone on the other side right now seeing her hand, broken into pieces like a kaleidoscope? She turned her head, her left eye straining, but all she could see was the blurry starfish of her fingers.

What was on the other side of this window? She traced its outlines, stopping when she found a divide in the middle at about eye level. And, her fingers told her, a lock shaped like a half moon. Something inside her loosened a tiny bit when she tried the lock and it swiveled. She had hoped for this and feared it in equal measures.

In her head, Cheyenne reconstructed the twists and turns they had taken since leaving the car. It was a skill she had learned in the last three years. Before she had lost her sight, she could barely be counted on to remember left or right. After the accident, one of the first things the orientation and mobility instructor had taught Cheyenne was to always, always, always orient herself using cardinal directions.

Now it was second nature, like a computer program running in the background, there when she needed to know whether she was facing east, west, south, or north. She had gotten out of the car and felt the sun at her back. So that had been east, because at that point the sun was still rising.

They had walked more or less due west to the house. A bedroom was at the back of the house—so even farther west—and next to it was the bathroom in which she now stood.

On the other side of this window, there was—what? Not the men, not the power tools, not the driveway. That was all on the other side of the house. Probably no neighbors, or Griffin wouldn't have let her walk around outside with her hands tied behind her. The air ahead of them had been silent and still. No sounds, no smells except the scent of pine needles.

Who knew if anyone was watching her now or if a bush covered the window? Who knew that even if she managed to get out, she wouldn't immediately find an obstacle—that out-of-control dog, a barbed-wire fence, or a man with fists or even a gun? Who knew that Griffin wouldn't just break down the door, run to the window, and shoot her in the back?

There was no time to think, no time to hesitate. Cheyenne took a deep breath and slid the window up, praying that Griffin wouldn't hear the faint rattle over the water gurgling down the sink's drain. At the base of her throat, she could feel her heart pounding. She fought back the urge to cough. She tucked the trail of cord into her sock, so that it wouldn't catch on anything. Moving fast, Cheyenne put down the seat and lid on the toilet, climbed up, and braced her hands on the windowsill.

Running After a Figment

Cheyenne had been in the bathroom for a long time. But Griffin didn't want to hover outside. He didn't want to look all pervy. Instead, he paced back and forth in the hall.

Finally, he knocked softly on the door. No answer. He called her name and knocked louder.

Only then did he think of the window in the back of the bathroom. *Crap!* He tried to turn the knob, but it was locked. Griffin remembered hearing the lock click into place, remembered thinking she was modest for running the water, and knew that he had been played for a fool.

He slammed his shoulder into the door. The impact made his teeth clack together, but the door held firm. Bracing himself in the narrow hallway, he turned and kicked sideways at the door like a kung-fu guy he had seen on a TV movie. He kicked it once, twice, and then on the third try, something snapped and the door swung open.

A blast of cold air hit him in the face. So cold it was a wonder it hadn't seeped under the door and alerted him to what she had done. The bathroom window gaped open. He ran to it and looked out. Outside, everything was still. There wasn't even a breeze to ruffle the pine needles. The woods began about twenty feet from the house. He hadn't left her in the bathroom that long. Even in a worst-case scenario, even if Cheyenne had gone deep into the woods, he should still be able to hear her crashing through the underbrush. Instead it was quiet.

How could that be? But he had already noticed how sure-footed she was, placing each foot as carefully as a cat, drawing back whenever she felt something that wasn't quite right.

Even if he couldn't see her, she couldn't have gotten very far. The quicker he went after her, the quicker he would catch her. His half-formed plan was to bring her back, tie her up again, and convince her not to say anything to Roy. If his dad found out, Roy would beat Griffin black and blue. And probably Cheyenne as well. And that was if Griffin found Cheyenne and brought her back. If he didn't find her—well, he didn't like to think about what would happen then.

He had to hurry and find her before she hurt herself. It would be harder to keep the whole thing a secret if she came back all scratched up. A branch could catch her in the throat or poke her in the eye. She could sprain her ankle on the uneven ground.

Right now she must be moving as fast as she could through the woods, knowing that the only thing she had on her side was a little bit of time. Griffin felt a grudging respect.

He stepped up on the toilet seat and grabbed the casement. He was just swinging his leg out when the faintest of sounds made him look toward the tub. Now that he was two feet off the ground, he could just see over the blue shower curtain with its faded green and yellow seahorses.

And what he saw was Cheyenne, crouched in the tub. Hiding behind the shower curtain.

Her hand was pressed to her mouth, and her face was tilted up. Her eyes seemed to be looking right at him, and it was the oddest thing to see her expression not change when he looked back at her. She wasn't completely still. A fine tremble was washing over her body, so that she almost looked as if she were vibrating. He could tell that she was listening with every fiber of her being. Waiting for him to leap out the window and go running after a figment of his imagination. While she did—what? Found a phone and locked herself in a room? Ran out the front door and tried to find the road? Even hid in the house, figuring they would never look for her there?

As he balanced, half in and half out of the window, staring at Cheyenne, Griffin heard the sound of two cars, one right after the other, cutting through the crystalline air. He identified them as the Honda and the pickup, which was almost as bad as if it had been Roy's Suburban. TJ and Jimbo were back.

In a few minutes, the two men would be in the house, wanting to ogle Cheyenne, wanting to talk about what they had seen at the shopping mall, wanting to boast about their bravery in retrieving the Honda.

In a single movement, Griffin pulled his leg back in and jumped, not out the window, but into the tub. With a sound like firecrackers, the shower curtain rings popped as the curtain ripped away under his weight. Underneath the damp, sour-smelling plastic, Cheyenne twisted frantically. He wrapped his arms around her muffled form. While he still could, before the engines cut out and the two men made their way into the house, he risked shouting at her.

"Listen to me!" He shoved her back against the tiled wall. Her head made a hollow thunk. "Listen! In a minute, those guys will be in here. And if they know you were trying to escape, they'll tell Roy. And he'll make our lives a living hell." He gave her another shake for emphasis. "Both our lives. Do you want to get beat up and hog-tied? Do you?"

The shower curtain slid down from her face. Her lips were pulled back in a snarl. "I know your name. It's Griffin. And now I know for sure that your dad's name is Roy. When I tell the police that, they'll find you in a minute."

He grabbed her upper arms, hard, and he didn't slacken his grip, even when Cheyenne cried out in pain.

"Do you just want to die?" Griffin hissed. "Is that it? You

start pointing stuff like that out to my dad, he's not going to feel like letting you go."

Inside, he was shaking. Every second it seemed like all the choices got worse and worse. And there was no way to undo what he had done. If only he had spent two seconds checking in the backseat! A two-second mistake was going to destroy his life. Cheyenne was right, Griffin knew. If Roy let her go, the police would find them without too much trouble. And then what?

Suddenly, she went slack. "All right," she said, her voice low. "Help me get out of here and then you can tie me back up. Quick."

He hustled her out of the bathroom—closing the door on the tattletale ripped shower curtain—and then back into his room. He pulled the cord that was tied around her ankle out of her sock and quickly looped it around the bedpost. What about her hands? He had cut off the shoelaces, and the remainder of the cord he had used to tie her ankle was out on the kitchen counter. Griffin had taken two steps to get it when he heard the front door open.

He barely had time to turn back and hiss, "Quick—put your hands behind your back!" before TJ and Jimbo were thumping down the hall.

"You should've seen it!" Jimbo crowed. He had added a black down vest over his coat. Griffin wondered how he had been able to fit behind the steering wheel. "That place was crawling with cops. And they had two of those portable news vans there with reporters doing stand-ups. One was that hot redhead on Channel Three. And they had yellow crime-scene tape up around a bunch of parking spaces—must have been where the Escalade was parked."

"Where's R—" TJ started, then said, "Ow!" when Jimbo elbowed him. "Why'd you do that?" he protested.

"No names, dummy." Jimbo nodded in Cheyenne's direction. "No names and she'll never know who we are."

It infuriated Griffin that Jimbo was capable of thinking further ahead than he had been. "He's gone to make some phone calls," Griffin said. He risked a glance at Cheyenne. She was sitting with her back against the headboard, her arms tucked behind her as if they were still lashed together. Every time someone spoke, her head swiveled in that direction. He wondered if that was left over from being able to see, or if it helped her hear better.

"There was this other lady there, too, and people were lining up to interview her. Must have been your mama," Jimbo said to Cheyenne.

"Her stepmom." Griffin found himself correcting him.

"Did her real mom get herself traded in for a better model?" TJ said. " 'Cause that Nike president's got himself a nice piece of ass."

"Don't talk like that around her," Griffin said sharply. He could see how stiffly Cheyenne held herself.

Jimbo and TJ responded at the same time with a mocking "ooh!"

"How much money do you think he'll want to spend to get his own daughter back?" Jimbo said. "A million?" Griffin heard the yearning in his voice.

TJ reached out to finger Cheyenne's curls. "A pretty thing like you ought to go for a lot."

Cheyenne's lips curled back. She jerked her head away from TJ. But when she did, she lost her balance and had to put out one hand to stop from tipping over. A hand that was obviously not tied to anything at all.

"Well, well, well, what have we here?" Jimbo said. "How come you don't have her tied up?"

One Way to Describe Stealing

Something dark loomed in the corner of Cheyenne's vision as the gross one taunted her. When she instinctively pulled back, her hand flew up, revealing that she was no longer tied up. She froze. What excuse would Griffin give? Five minutes earlier, she had been ready to scratch his eyes out. Now he seemed like the only buffer between her and these men who treated her like she didn't have ears to hear what they said.

Griffin sounded unhurried, unworried. "She had to go to the bathroom. I was just getting ready to tie her back up when you guys came home."

"Are you sure that's all that's been happening?" the gross guy said. "I mean, maybe you're just taking advantage of the fact that you finally got a girl in your bed."

So this was Griffin's room, not a guest room. Cheyenne was surprised.

"Better not handle the merchandise," the other man said. He seemed smarter, but not by much. "Remember, you break it, you bought it."

Wanting to keep the focus away from her untied wrists, Cheyenne put the hand that was no longer behind her back in her pocket. She barely missed cutting herself on the piece of glass she had hidden there earlier. It was nestled in the kibble that always, since she had gotten Phantom, half filled her pockets. (Cheyenne had learned the hard way to check before she put her clothes in the washer.) The kibble was used for rewards, as well as for what the guide dog school had called counter-conditioning. If Phantom was distracted, giving him a piece of kibble was one sure way to get his attention back on her.

"Bring me the twine," the second man said. "Let somebody who knows what he's doing tie her up."

The gross one sniggered.

For a minute, Cheyenne wondered if she could use the glass to hold them all at bay. And then what? She couldn't come up with a scenario that lasted for more than a few seconds. It probably wasn't even possible to cut someone with a broken piece of glass without cutting yourself at the same time.

"I've got things under control," Griffin said. "And it's not like she's some huge flight risk. She's blind, remember? You guys should go out and finish working on that Toyota."

Nobody moved. There wasn't a sound. She wished she

knew what was happening. In the silence, she could feel the tension stretching out between Griffin and the two men.

Then the second man laughed. "You just think you got things under control." But there was a note in his tone, as if he were trying to save face, trying to make Griffin think this was his decision, not Griffin's.

Cheyenne and Griffin were both silent until they heard the front door open and close. Then she said, "Thanks. I don't like them."

"You're not the only one."

"Who are they?" Cheyenne made a conscious effort to look toward his face. People got nervous if you didn't look at them, but for her, the face was no longer important. It was just the place the voice came from.

"Guys who work for my dad."

"Doing what, exactly?" *What kind of employees would just accept it if you showed up with a kidnapped girl?*

Griffin hesitated for so long she wondered if he was even going to answer. Finally, he said, "We sell cars and car parts for cheaper. Say you want to buy a seat for a Honda Civic. If you get it from the dealer, it'll cost you three thousand. Buy it off us, it's a lot cheaper. A lot."

"So why is it so much cheaper?" Now that the two men were gone, Cheyenne's body was reminding her how sick she was. She had used up all her energy thinking about how to escape, then deciding it would be better to try to find a phone once the house was empty, and then struggling with Griffin. "Do you guys run a wrecking yard or something?"

"Or something." Griffin sighed and settled down on the end of the bed. Cheyenne pulled her feet farther back so that she wouldn't touch him. "It's a little bit of this and a little bit of that." He took a deep breath. "One of the things we do is buy junker cars at auction. Stuff that the insurance company has declared a total loss."

"And you use them for parts?"

"Mostly we just use a couple of the parts, and that's it. Just the ones with the VIN on them."

"What's a VIN?"

"The vehicle identification number. VINs are like Social Security numbers, only for your car. Each car has a different one. There's a tiny one on every dashboard that you can see through the windshield, but they put them in a few other places, too. The cops can check a VIN to see if a car has been stolen. So once we buy a junker, then we go looking for a second car that's the exact same year, make, and model, only not totaled."

Cheyenne thought she knew where this was going. "And you don't buy that other car, do you?"

"No. We steal it. Then we put the VINs from the junker on the stolen car, and we end up with a car with a clear title and a perfectly legal VIN. We register it with a phony name and address and then resell it to someone who isn't going to ask too many questions about why they're getting a nice car a couple of thousand under Kelley Blue Book."

"But it's stolen!"

"You really think the person who buys it doesn't have any idea?" Griffin snorted. "They know. They just don't want to know. If you know what I mean."

"So is that why you stole the Escalade—you have a trashed one sitting around someplace that you can use the VINs from?"

Cheyenne could hear the reluctance in his reply. "Uh, that was more like an accident. Normally, we get the junker first and then steal the better car. And I don't usually take cars. J—" He stopped himself from saying someone's name, but she filed away the initial. "The other guys do that. I just saw the keys in the ignition and I acted on impulse. Obviously. Or I would have noticed that you were in the back. My dad's not real happy with me right now."

"So what are you going to do with Danielle's car? Buy a damaged one and switch out the VINs?" But it would always be her family's car, Cheyenne thought. The one with the inch-long scratch on the passenger's side where Phantom's rigid steel harness had caught the first week she had him.

"It's a sweet ride, but right now it's a little too hot, even if we put on new VINs and new plates. They'll be stopping every car like it from Seattle to San Francisco. The radio said they've got an AMBER Alert out for you. We might just have to part it out, you know, and sell a piece here and a piece there, but not the whole car. A bumper from a car like that might cost four thousand new from the dealer. We could cut a car repair place a deal for half the price and still come out ahead, since we got the car for free."

For free. Cheyenne guessed that was one way to describe stealing. "But what about the VIN? Won't they know the bumper came from our car?"

"They don't put the VIN on every part, so once you take a part away from the car, the cops can't trace it. There's a lot of body shops that will look the other way and buy stuff from us. They save money, and we make money. So everybody's happy."

"Except the guy who just paid a lot for a stolen bumper. Or the person whose whole car has been turned into a pile of parts."

She could hear his shrug. "My dad says that's what insurance is for."

"But what about—" Cheyenne started to argue, only the words caught in her throat. Then she was doubled over coughing, trying to catch her breath.

Griffin brought her some more water, but she waved it away, still coughing. Finally it was done.

"Are you okay?"

Maybe she was imagining it, but she thought there was real concern in Griffin's voice.

"Not really. Could you maybe just let me sleep?" It was

all she could do to hold her head up and have this conversation.

"Sure."

She had one last waking thought. "Just keep those guys
away from me."

14

Hung for a Sheep

Figuring he had better do it before his dad got back, Griffin tied Cheyenne's ankle more tightly to the bed. She barely stirred, her head pillowed on her forearm. She looked exhausted. Except for her flushed cheeks, her face was as white as paper. Griffin got a blue-and-pink quilt (his grandma had made it when his mother was pregnant with him but didn't know if he was a boy or a girl) from the hall closet and gently draped it over Cheyenne. It smelled kind of musty, but he wanted her to be warm.

In a way, it had been a relief to talk to Cheyenne about Roy's business. At first Griffin had considered not answering her question about what his dad did, or lying. But what was it his grandma used to say before she stopped making sense? Might as well be hung for a sheep as a lamb, that was it. Meaning, if you were already screwed, then what the hell. Cheyenne already knew too much, so what was a little bit more?

Besides, he had never talked about it to anyone. Griffin had felt a strange sense of pride as he had described the various tricks they used to turn something illegal into something legal or something that nobody wanted into something that somebody did. He had kept on talking, even when it was clear she was barely staying awake. It had been like trying to stop the air from leaking out of a punctured balloon. He wished he had thought to tell Cheyenne about the "strip and run," his favorite trick. TJ or Jimbo would steal a car, strip its parts, and then abandon what was left. Eventually, the police would recover the vehicle and cancel the theft record. Then Roy would purchase the frame at an insurance auction and tow it home. In the barn, the stolen parts would be reattached to the very same car they had come from. The end result was a whole, valuable, and perfectly legal car that Roy could sell for many times more than he had paid for the stripped frame.

Thinking about stolen stuff reminded Griffin that there was still a trunk load of loot from the shopping center in the Honda. But there was no way he was going to leave Cheyenne here alone to go sell it on Eighty-second in Portland, even if she hadn't begged him to watch over her. Griffin didn't think TJ was anything more than talk, but there were times when Jimbo found a way of goading TJ into action. If it worked out, Jimbo would join in. If it didn't, Jimbo stepped back and let TJ take the blame.

As he gently closed the door to his bedroom, Griffin

wondered when his dad would come back and what he would say when he did. He reached into his pocket for his cigarettes as he walked into the kitchen. Ever since he had brought Cheyenne inside, he had seen the house with new eyes. And what he saw was depressing, shabby, and dirty. It didn't matter that Cheyenne would never actually see it. He slid the cigarette pack back into his shirt pocket, then emptied the sink, filled it with hot, soapy water, and went to work.

Two hours later, the dishes were drying in the rack and the kitchen floor had been mopped until it shone. Griffin had a sudden appreciation for what it must have been like for his mom. No wonder she had left. Two hours of work, and he knew it could all be undone in a few minutes. Still, he had a feeling of satisfaction. The mail, old newspapers, and random auto parts that had covered the dining room table had been either sorted into neat piles on the sideboard, taken out to the burn barrel, or put away in the barn. Whenever Griffin went outside, TJ and Jimbo didn't seem to be working much, just leaning on half-dismantled cars, their breath clouding the air, talking and gesturing toward the house. They shut up whenever he got near enough to hear what they were saying.

Before he turned his attention to the living room, he softly opened the door to check on Cheyenne, as he already had a half-dozen times. This time she was awake and sitting up.

"It's ten to five," she said. He wondered how she knew that, then saw her click the face of her watch closed. "Please—can we watch the local news? I want to see if it says anything about me." She looked better, but her voice was still hoarse.

"See?" he echoed. "Is it okay to say that around you?"

Something like a smile twisted her mouth. "People get too hung up on that. It's not like if they don't use it I'm going to forget that I'm blind. My dad even tries not to say he's going to see me later. I keep telling him that *see* is just a word. Everyone uses it. I use it all the time." She paused, and then said in a rush, "I remember what it was like to see. Sometimes I still think I can. When I first wake up in the morning, part of me thinks that when I open my eyes I'll see my room, you know, or what's outside my window. And I still imagine what everything looks like."

Cheyenne's face, although still pale, was animated. Griffin kind of liked that he could watch her for as long as he wanted and that she wouldn't mind. But whenever her gaze—or what seemed to be her gaze—touched his, he noticed that he still looked away, just as if she *could* see.

Suddenly bold, he asked, "What do I look like, then?"

"You?"

He flushed and was glad she couldn't see him. "Never mind."

She continued as if he hadn't said anything. "Let's see. You're about five foot eleven, one hundred seventy pounds.

Strong. I think your hair must be dark. You just *sound* like you have dark hair. And for some reason I think you must have a big nose. I mean, it's not a little nubbin, it's not a girly nose."

He stared in surprise. She was right—right about everything she had said, anyway. The height and weight shouldn't have been too hard to get, not after he had wrestled with her twice today. Maybe she had even bumped into his nose. He remembered her scratching his face. It was weird, but as she described him, Griffin had expected her to mention the ugly red ribbon of scar that wrapped around his neck.

"What about me?" Cheyenne asked. "What do I look like?"

He was taken aback. "Um, don't you know?"

She shrugged. "I haven't seen myself in a mirror for three years. I don't have any idea what I look like anymore. The last time I saw myself I was thirteen."

Was she flirting with him? Cheyenne's face was open and innocent. Of course, she had worn the same expression when she claimed she had to go to the bathroom. He looked at her dark curls, her olive skin, her heart-shaped face.

"You're pretty," he said in a voice that didn't invite any questions. "You're pretty, okay?" He realized he was clenching his fists.

For a second, Cheyenne looked surprised, and then she

wiped all expression from her face. "The news should be starting on TV now," she said. "Please, can we watch it?"

Griffin wondered if this was a trick on her part. Maybe she just wanted to be in another part of the house so that she could find a phone. He let the silence stretch out long enough that she would appreciate how much she was asking of him. "Okay," he finally said, "but I'm going to have to tie you to the couch. And if my dad comes in and starts yelling, you have to promise to be quiet and follow my lead, okay?"

"Promise," she said, and made a gesture like she was crossing her heart.

He untied her ankle and then held on to the cord as he took her elbow and walked her into the living room. Once Cheyenne stumbled when she tried to take a step longer than the cord would allow. "Sorry," he said, grabbing her elbow just in time to prevent her from falling over the coffee table. It was actually a giant wooden spool that had once held wire cable. He maneuvered her so that the couch was just behind her knees. "You can sit down."

Griffin tied her ankle to one of the clawed feet of the old couch, glad she couldn't see the stains on the cushions. As a safety measure, he reached over and unplugged the phone from the wall. Then he sat on the couch, picked up the clicker, and punched in the number for one of the local stations.

After a commercial for some kind of adult diaper—Griffin

most definitely didn't want to get old—the female announcer appeared on the screen, looking somber. Above her left shoulder a little box showed a photograph of yellow crime-scene tape. "In tonight's top story, the parents of a girl taken today from the Woodlands Experience shopping center have made a heartrending appeal for her safe return. Channel Eight's Tami Engel spoke late this afternoon with Nick and Danielle Wilder, the parents of sixteen-year-old Cheyenne Wilder."

The TV cut away to a man with a tan face and dark hair that was silver at the temples. Beside him was a blond woman with what Griffin thought of as an expensive haircut, spiky at the edges, with lighter and darker streaks mixed in. They were seated on a dark brown leather couch. Behind them was a rustic stone fireplace, and next to the fireplace towered a huge Christmas tree, decorated all in silver. Griffin figured it was the Wilders' house, but he wondered if it was such a good idea for them to be filmed there. The whole place screamed "money." And if Roy saw this—when Roy saw this—he would probably double Cheyenne's asking price.

When Mr. Wilder started speaking, Griffin felt Cheyenne jump.

"I will do anything that's necessary to get my precious daughter back," Mr. Wilder said. "People can call me twenty-four hours a day if they know something." The camera zoomed in on his face, wet with tears. The tears and the tan didn't go together. "We need to bring my little girl back home right away. Just imagine how terrifying it is for her. My daughter is blind!"

The blond woman laid a hand on her husband's arm. "Cheyenne is a strong person. I'm sure she'll get through this." Then she sighed heavily. "I feel so guilty. I insisted she not take her guide dog with her. I just thought it would be easier. Now I keep thinking, 'If only she had had Phantom with her, this would never have happened.' " She covered her face. From behind her hands came a strangled noise.

"Is she crying?" Cheyenne asked.

"Yeah. So's your dad."

For the second time in a single day, Griffin thought of his own mom, something he seldom allowed himself to do. How would she have reacted? Would she have cried? Or would she have looked out for herself, the way she had seven years earlier?

Cheyenne said in a voice that seemed more for her own ears, "I've never seen Danielle cry before."

The camera switched back to Mr. Wilder. "Cheyenne is very sick," he said to the reporter, who nodded sympathetically. "She was diagnosed with pneumonia right before she was kidnapped, and she needs to be on antibiotics. I'm begging these people to let her go immediately. How can they take a girl like that, a helpless child? She must be so frightened." He turned and spoke directly to the camera. "As a father, I beg you, I beg you, look at Cheyenne's face. Please, please don't hurt her, let her go." His voice turned hard. "And know this—if you harm one hair on my daughter's head, I'll come after you myself."

The reporter, Tami, leaned forward. "Do you think this is related to your being president of Nike?"

Cheyenne's father nodded. The tears were gone from his face now. "It's likely. It's no secret that my daughter means everything to me. They could have been watching, waiting for a time when she was vulnerable. As my wife said, she didn't have her guide dog with her this morning."

Then he addressed Cheyenne directly. "Cheyenne, I know we are physically separated, but my heart"—his words stumbled and broke—"my heart has never separated from you, not for a moment, not for a second. Please be strong. We will get you home soon."

Griffin looked at Cheyenne. She was trembling so hard it was as if she were about to fly apart. Tears were now running down her cheeks, but when she spoke, her tone was angry and agitated. "I thought your dad was going to ask for a ransom. How come they're not saying that they've heard from the kidnappers and are considering their demands? They're talking like they don't know anything!"

"I don't know." Griffin raised his voice to match hers. "I have no idea. I've been with you, remember? Maybe my dad wasn't able to get through to them."

The announcer was saying, "Police have released few details about the case, but have suggested Cheyenne Wilder may have been kidnapped for ransom. There is no evidence this was the random act of a sexual predator. Right before we went on air, officials told us they have received over a hundred tips so far, and each one is being pursued. The Wilders' phone is constantly ringing, and they are receiving hundreds of e-mails. The police are concentrating on leads from the public. So if you were at Woodlands today around ten A.M. and may have seen a green Escalade, license plate 396 CVS, please call a special hotline that has been set up, 1-888-555-1212. Here's a picture of Cheyenne with her dog, Phantom." The TV cut away to a photo of Cheyenne, grinning. Even the dog, a golden lab, seemed to be grinning. Before he had dropped out of school, Griffin had learned there was a word for that, a word for thinking that animals had the same emotions as humans.

Griffin couldn't remember the word anymore.

And Griffin knew that he would never see Cheyenne grin like she was in the photo. As he stared at her wide smile, the announcer concluded with, "The race is on to find Cheyenne Wilder and to rescue her alive."

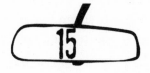

Might as Well Be Dead

Cheyenne snapped her head around to face the front door.

"What's the matter?" Griffin asked.

"Someone's here." The car she had begun hearing a few seconds earlier pulled up outside the house, fast enough that gravel scattered in its wake. Maybe it was someone coming to rescue her. She remembered the gun that Griffin had. Would he take her hostage? Cheyenne scooted to the far end of the couch, trying to get out of reach.

"Crap—is it my dad?" He clicked off the TV.

She heard a car door open and close. Then people talking. Just as quickly as they had bubbled up, her hopes burst. Although she couldn't make out the words, Cheyenne recognized the voices—it was Griffin's dad and the two men who worked for him. Quickly, she rubbed her scarf over her face. She didn't want anyone to see her tears. But it was a minute before they came in. She thought she heard another car door close. Finally, steps on the wooden porch. The door crashed open, and a cold wind blew over them.

"Fraternizing with the enemy?" Roy said. He sounded, Cheyenne thought, drunk. The other two men laughed.

Cheyenne was as tight as a guitar string.

"Hey." Griffin was trying too hard to sound casual. "Um, how'd it go?"

Instead of answering Griffin, Roy said, "This is your cane, right?" She heard him give it a shake. He must have retrieved it from the Escalade.

There was the sound of metal grating on metal, a groan as some kind of door opened. Heat washed through the room. Cheyenne heard fluttering flames, smelled wood smoke.

Roy said, "We don't need to leave anything around that might come in handy for you." And then she heard him throw the cane inside the stove. The door clanged closed.

For so long, Cheyenne had hated her cane. Canes were for old people. Handicapped people. Not teenagers. Not for people like her. But now as the smell of the smoke changed, she felt lost. Her cane was made of fiberglass, so it might not burn, but the elastic cord that held the sections together certainly would, turning it into a useless bundle of rods.

"What happened? What's the matter?" Griffin's voice sounded higher pitched. Scared.

"Not in front of her. What's she doing out here, anyway?" Roy didn't wait for an answer. She could hear him pacing back and forth. "Put her back in your room. Then we need to talk."

Griffin hustled Cheyenne away. He tied her ankle to the bed but left her hands free. "Sorry," he said. She wasn't sure, but she thought she felt his hand brush the top of her hair. She felt oddly reluctant for him to leave. Who would come through the door next? Griffin might be bad, but she knew the other three men were worse. And why was Roy so angry?

What had happened? Had her parents refused to pay a ransom? But that was impossible. Even before she heard him on TV, Cheyenne had known her dad would do anything to get her back.

Maybe while she had been napping, Griffin had called Roy with the news about her escape attempt. Was that why he had thrown her cane into the woodstove?

Smoke from the elastic cord still hung in the air, and Cheyenne started to cough. Echoing, wet, tearing coughs, like she was going to cough up one of her lungs. When it finally stopped, she was covered with a light sheen of sweat, even though Griffin's room was cold. She found the quilt and pulled it over her. There was nothing else to do. She closed her eyes.

Using a cane had been the first skill Cheyenne had had to learn after the accident, and the hardest. Her dad hadn't wanted to let her go to the residential program, but Danielle had persuaded him. That was before Cheyenne's dad and

Danielle started dating, before Danielle became her step-mother, back when she was just one of the voices of the nice nurses who cared for Cheyenne.

Although in Danielle's case, not so nice. Danielle hadn't believed in spending too much time mourning what was lost. Instead she wanted Cheyenne to focus on what she *had*, on what she *could* do.

For the first two months after the accident, Cheyenne was basically in bed. First, it was because her broken body needed to heal. After the initial ten days, when she was out of danger, the hospital recommended that she be sent to a nursing home to recuperate. Her father wouldn't hear of it—his thirteen-year-old daughter surrounded by old people with strokes and broken hips? Instead, he paid for private-duty nurses to be with her twenty-four hours a day. One of them was Danielle.

Once Cheyenne realized that she would never see again, she shut down. What was the point? The world was a scary place. The physical therapist wanted her to go to a special school where she would learn how to be blind. Cheyenne said no to everything, and her dad didn't argue. She didn't like to get out of bed. There was nothing around her, and how could she walk on nothing? If Cheyenne had to go someplace, she slid her feet as if she were on roller skates, so that she could still have one foot on the world.

All she had left for sure was her body, trembling and sweating. The churning in her stomach, the pounding in her temples, the sounds of her breathing. She no longer knew anything about the world. All she knew about was herself. Her world had shrunk to the edges of her skin.

Every time her dad encouraged her to get up, Cheyenne complained that her head ached or that she felt dizzy. Sometimes it was even true. Sometimes she didn't know if it was true or not. Mostly she stayed in bed and listened to music. Her dad would stand in the door of her room watching her—she could hear him, even if he didn't always say he was there—and Cheyenne would just turn her music up louder.

Then one day Danielle popped the headphones out of her ears.

"Hey!" Cheyenne protested. Her hands scrabbled over the bedcovers, trying to find them.

"Listen," Danielle said, her voice brisk and matter-of-fact, "this is going to be one long, boring life if you don't learn how to function independently. At this rate, you might as well be dead."

Cheyenne had held it together so well for weeks, but now she snapped. She was tired of sympathy, but this woman's expectations were way out of line.

"Might as well be dead? I am dead! I'll never see anything again—not a movie, not a person's face, not even my own face." She bogged down thinking of all the things she wouldn't see—flowers and dogs and the colors of her clothes and sunsets, leaves turning, TV shows and books, concerts, cute boys, cute actors, cute babies, what exactly was making a strange noise, the colors of gelato and the shiny metal tubs they were lined up in, cracks in the sidewalk, people laughing at her.

Danielle's voice remained calm. "You're only thirteen. You've got your whole life ahead of you."

"Don't give me any of that crap about how I'm only thirteen. My life is over. I'm never going to drive a car, I'm never going to go on a date, and I'll be lucky if I get a job in some shelter for the handicapped." Cheyenne made her voice singsongy, furious that she could still hear the tears underneath. "I'm sick of people saying 'you're still young,' 'you'll adapt,' 'God never closes a door but he opens a window.' Well, that's all BS! I won't adapt. I'm blind. My mom's dead and I'm blind!"

There was a long pause. Then Danielle said quietly, "You're right. But it is what it is, Cheyenne. You can't change it, so you have to deal with it. You have to figure out how to do things for yourself. You *can* make a life. And it can be a good one. But you have to try."

From outside Cheyenne's closed door, her dad called, "What are you girls talking about in there?"

"Go away!" Cheyenne shouted. She didn't want him to see her with tears spilling out of her useless eyes. Then he would start crying too. She didn't want another pity party. She just wanted to forget. She just wanted to go to sleep and wake up and have it all be a bad dream.

She waited until she heard her father's footsteps turn away. Then she said softly, "But it's too much. It's just too much."

Danielle was relentless. "Aren't you getting tired of living like a baby? Of having everyone do everything for you? Don't you want to learn how to do some things for yourself?"

It was true. Cheyenne was starting to feel like a baby trapped in a thirteen-year-old body. Sometimes her dad even fed her.

She kept still for a long time and then, slowly, she nodded. She felt Danielle settle on the bed beside her. Her arms went around Cheyenne. For a second, Cheyenne stiffened, and then she let herself be rocked back and forth while Danielle made *sh-sh* sounds in her ear.

That was how her dad had found them. Later, after Danielle and her dad told Cheyenne they were getting married, she wondered if Danielle hadn't somehow planned being found like that. To show that she could take Cheyenne's mom's place.

Still, Danielle hadn't been wrong. And because of her encouragement, Cheyenne had learned how to do a lot of things for herself, more than she had ever thought possible in the first horrible weeks after the accident. Most of what she had learned had been at a residential school two hours from her home.

Many of the people there were like Cheyenne, in shock,

wondering what had happened to them. She remembered in particular one guy who kept saying, "But how will I be able to do things if I can't drive?" After a while, she wanted to slug him. He was forty at least, so he had had a life. He had had his chance. Cheyenne hadn't even really gotten started. Her mom had let her drive once in a cemetery near their house, but now she would never get to for real. And her mom was buried in that same cemetery. Cheyenne had never even been to her grave.

At first when she was at the school, Cheyenne had felt like an alien who had just landed on the planet. She had had to relearn things that she had known how to do for so long that she didn't remember not knowing them. How to feed herself. How to dress herself. How to walk without bumping into things.

One of the first things she learned was how to use a cane. Surprisingly light, the cane had a rubber handle like a golf club and a plastic tip. The cane could be folded up into a neat little bundle of sticks. Cheyenne resolved to keep it folded up and hidden away as much as possible. When the instructors told her it glowed in the dark, she imagined how it would give her away at night, the one time she might have a slight advantage over sighted people.

Still, while she was at the school, surrounded by other blind people, she decided to learn how to use it. Danielle had told Cheyenne a Bible verse, "For we walk by faith, not by sight." Using a cane was like that. Each step was like stepping into nothing until she felt solid ground under her feet again.

It made a *tacka-tacka* sound. "Touch, don't tap," the instructors said. They taught her how to sweep it from side to side like a metal detector, touching the spot where the next foot would land. When she stepped forward to the left, she tapped on the right. If there was a hole, or something in her way, the cane would find it first. Going down stairs, she held her cane directly in front of her and learned to trust that it would tap when she reached the bottom. Through the feedback she got from the cane, Cheyenne learned to feel grates, ups, downs, carpeting, tile, wood, gravel, curbs, grass, and swishing revolving doors.

And she learned that it wasn't just that the cane could tell her what was directly in her path. If she listened closely, she could tell whether the sound it made was bouncing off a brick wall or echoing in an open doorway or rebounding off an awning overhead. Even without the cane, she could sometimes tell if there was something ahead of her, like a tree or a telephone pole. As a blind person, Cheyenne had to interpret every shred of information she could get from her other senses. Everyone thought the blind had special abilities, but it was really that they had just learned to pay attention. That they *had* to pay attention.

Now as she lay on Griffin's bed, Cheyenne remembered the first time the instructors had had her venture out on her own. She had walked down a city street, listening to other people's footsteps around her, fearful she might hit one of them with her cane. (That was before she realized that a cane was good for crowd control—once they saw it, people usually gave her a wide berth.) She wondered if they were staring. At one point, she thought she heard someone whispering, but she told herself she was imagining it. After a couple of blocks, her breath finally began to come easier.

"Are you blind?" someone asked, startling her. The voice belonged to a young boy.

Cheyenne turned, not sure she was looking in the right direction. She took a deep breath and let it out. "Yes."

"You must be really bad!" Then she heard the sound of his footsteps running away.

At the end of each day—she was there for three months, coming home only on weekends—Cheyenne had fallen into bed and slept so hard she didn't even dream. In some ways she was glad. In other ways she wished desperately to spend time with her mother again, even if it was only in a dream. The few times she did dream about her mother, Cheyenne was always searching through a huge crowd, only to finally catch just a glimpse as her mom left a room.

When the yelling began outside Griffin's door, Cheyenne was so deeply asleep she didn't hear it.

You Want Proof, I'll Give You Proof

Griffin hurried back into the living room. "What's wrong?" He hadn't seen his dad this angry for a long, long time. Back then, his mom had been around to try to jolly Roy out of it. Not that she usually succeeded.

For once, TJ and Jimbo were quiet, watching Roy with a look they normally reserved for Duke.

"Nothing," his dad snarled. He had taken the bottle of Maker's Mark out of the kitchen cupboard. He took a swallow of the whiskey and then looked at the two men who worked for him. "How come you're still hanging around? How come you're not at home?"

Jimbo knew enough to keep quiet, but not TJ. He said, "Because we wanted to hear what her folks said. How long till we get the money? How much are we going to get?"

"Who said anything about 'we'?" Roy roared. "It's my stupid kid who brought her back to my house. I'm the one who'll take the fall if this thing goes south. *When* this thing goes south. You guys can turn state's witness and come out of this smelling sweeter than a rose."

"But—" TJ *really* didn't know when to shut up.

"But nothing. Go home. Now." Roy took another slug, then wiped his mouth with the back of his hand. "We'll talk about it tomorrow."

"Can we just see her?" TJ asked.

"No," Griffin said firmly. "She needs to rest."

"Did you tucker her out?" TJ asked with a leer. "Come on, let TJ take a little peek. She's one sweet thing."

Griffin took two steps so that he stood between them and the hallway. "You heard Roy—go home."

TJ looked at him in surprise. He didn't back away, but he didn't go forward, either.

Jimbo was the one who finally showed some sense. "Come on, Teej, let's go. It sounds like nothing else is going to happen tonight."

"Dad, what's the matter?" Griffin asked after the door closed behind them. "They showed her parents on TV"— he decided to leave out the part about just how nice the house was—"and they said no one had contacted them. Didn't you call them?"

Roy looked away. "It took me a while to score a cell phone that I could use. And then when I finally had it, I couldn't find the piece of paper with the numbers on it."

Griffin felt confused. "What are you talking about?"

His father leaned forward until their faces were only inches apart and carefully enunciated each word. "I . . . lost . . . it." Griffin realized how bad Roy's mood really was. "I lost the goddamn slip of paper. So I couldn't call. I was trying to think of the best way to do this. So I was down at the Green Roof, making notes." The Green Roof Inn was a dive of a bar about twenty miles away, where Roy sometimes went to shoot pool and drink Pabst until he got kicked out for fighting. They always let him back in the next time, though, because if they barred all their customers for that type of behavior, they wouldn't have any left. "So, yeah, I watched those rich bastards on the TV above the bar. All"—he pitched his voice higher—"boo-hoo, my baby's gone." He switched back to his normal voice. "And then when I went out to the car to call them, I couldn't find the paper. Maybe they're just covering up. I mean, come on, it must be a drag, having to watch after this handicapped girl all the time. Maybe they want to get rid of her and start fresh."

"I think Cheyenne's pretty independent," Griffin said. He suddenly felt the need to defend her. "She's got a seeing-eye dog and everything." He paused, then said in a rush, "I've been thinking. Maybe we should just let her go. Without asking for money. And if the cops figured out who we were, which they probably wouldn't, we could explain it was all a mistake."

The blow to his belly came out of nowhere. The next

thing Griffin knew, he was on the floor, huddled up. The air was stuck somewhere inside him. His mouth opened like a fish hauled onto the bottom of a boat, but nothing came in and nothing went out. Time seemed to slow down and he could see everything—a paper clip on the carpet, the scuffs on the tips of Roy's work boots—with a kind of sparkling clarity. Was he going to die?

And then finally the air came rushing back in. It hurt just as bad as when it hadn't been there at all.

"Like that's such a bright idea." Roy leaned over him, shouting. "Like they're going to overlook what it is we do here?" With every word, spit freckled Griffin's face. "This chick could be our ticket out. On New Year's Eve, I want to be on a beach someplace warm, drinking mai tais. And now that could happen. But only if we play our cards absolutely right."

Griffin managed to sit up. He turned his head and rested his cheek against his bent knees.

"Sure, you screwed up when you didn't look in the backseat. But now that could be the best thing that ever happened to us. Go get her. I want to get those phone numbers again so I can talk to that fat-cat dad of hers."

Griffin had just learned—again—that it wasn't worth talking back to his dad. He got up and went in to get Cheyenne. She was asleep. When he touched her shoulder, she jerked awake, then pushed him away with both hands, her breathing rushed and panicky.

"Easy, easy," he said. "It's just me. My dad wants to talk to you."

"What did my parents say?" Looking both scared and excited, she sat up. "How come they acted like they hadn't talked to him yet?"

"Because they haven't. He needs you to give him the phone numbers again. He lost the paper that had them. But don't say nothing to him about it. He's in a real bad mood."

Cheyenne wiped her face clean of all expression and nodded. Griffin untied her ankle and walked her down the hall.

Holding a cell phone so big it was almost funny, Roy was waiting for them. "All right, what's your home number again?"

Cheyenne recited it in a dead voice.

Griffin watched his dad's expression as he listened to the phone ring. His face changed when someone answered.

"Listen," Roy barked. "I've got the girl. I've got Cheyenne Wilder. I'm offering you a trade. You give me money, and I'll give her back. It's that simple."

His eyes narrowed. "You want proof? I'll give you proof." Forgetting she was blind, he thrust the phone at Cheyenne. When she didn't take it, he swore and fumbled it into her hand. "Don't say anything stupid," he warned her.

"Daddy?" Her face changed. Suddenly she looked like a little kid. "Daddy?" She bit her lip at the answer. "Oh. I'm okay, but—"

"That's enough." Roy yanked the phone away from her and put it back to his ear. "I'm sure you got that taped. You run that through your computers or have her parents listen to it, and they'll tell you that I'm telling the truth. And you tell them we're gonna need five million dollars. Nothing larger than a fifty. Unmarked, nonconsecutive bills. Or you're gonna get her back in pieces!"

Griffin's mouth fell open. Five million? Geez, why hadn't his dad just asked for five hundred zillion quadrillion? Five million was impossible. Even if it was all in fifties, that would still be—he thought about it for a second—a hundred thousand bills. They would need a forklift for that.

"We'll be in touch," Roy said, almost jauntily. He clicked off the phone and gave Griffin a grin. His anger seemed to have evaporated. After seventeen years of living with him, Griffin knew that looks could be deceiving.

"That wasn't even my dad you had me talk to," Cheyenne told Roy. "Do you know that? That wasn't even my dad." Tears shone on her cheeks, but her voice didn't tremble at all.

Roy shrugged. "It was probably a cop. I heard a clicking on the line. They're probably trying to trace the phone. That's why I hung up, just to be on the safe side. Next time I call, I'll tell them to put the money into a bag and drop it off someplace we can watch to make sure that nobody's followed it. After we get the money, we'll check it out to make sure there's not a tracking device or dye on the bills. And then we'll let you go."

Cheyenne nodded. She looked like she didn't believe Roy.

Griffin didn't think he did, either.

For the first time, he had an unsettling thought.

Roy would eventually let Cheyenne go—wouldn't he?

Working in the Dark

Cheyenne swam out of a dream where she had been lost and running into things.

"Are you hungry?" Griffin asked from the doorway.

It took her a minute to orient herself. She was in a room in an old house in the middle of nowhere. Only four people knew where she was. And they were the ones who were holding her captive.

"Are you hungry?" Griffin asked again.

She wasn't hungry. She wasn't anything. She was empty. After her escape attempt had failed, Cheyenne had pinned her hopes on the idea that Griffin's dad was setting up a trade. She had told herself that she might even be home tonight. She had tried not to think about the details too much, intentionally kept them fuzzy. The only concession she had made to reality was to admit that maybe it might not happen until after midnight.

When Cheyenne still didn't answer, Griffin continued on as if she had. "I've got to get some food into my dad to balance out what he's had to drink. There's some frozen pizza I can heat up. How about that and some orange juice?" Griffin was forced to shout over the music that thumped in the living room, some kind of heavy metal that made her head hurt.

Cheyenne nodded. She pulled the quilt back over her and closed her eyes. She didn't need to do that for it to be dark, of course, but it was a way of signaling that she didn't want to talk anymore.

She half dozed until Griffin sat down on the edge of the bed and lifted the quilt away from her. "I thought I would eat in here with you."

As she pushed herself into a sitting position, Cheyenne could smell herself, the rank scents of fear and fever. It was strange how quickly things could become normal, she thought as she took the plate from Griffin's hand. She didn't like to be dirty or cold, she didn't like people telling her what to do, but here she was, feeling almost like it was an expected part of her routine. The same with the cord knotted around her ankle. She didn't even really notice it anymore. At least someone had turned down the music to a more tolerable level.

"There's a glass about six inches to the left of your elbow," Griffin said. "Um, at ten o'clock."

She picked up one of the two slices on her plate and

took a bite. Pepperoni, tasting mostly of salt and fat, with a big, pillowy crust. Danielle was really into healthy eating. She would be horrified by this pizza.

Cheyenne took another bite. Maybe she would be home by tomorrow. Maybe in twenty-four hours she would be just getting out of the shower and sliding between fresh sheets.

Griffin spoke around a mouthful of food. "What's it like being blind?"

"Do you think about what it's like to have hair every second?" Cheyenne blew air out of her nose. "It's just who I am now. I try not to think about it all the time." Which was true. But it didn't work. She never really forgot that she was blind. And even if she did for a minute, she could count on there being a reminder. Usually painful. She sighed. "At first, it feels like someone has thrown a blanket over your head. Some days you just want to scream, 'I'm inside here! Doesn't anybody out there see that? Doesn't anybody remember me? I'm still the same person!'" Cheyenne fell silent. She knew the last sentence wasn't true, even if she wanted it to be. She wasn't the same person. "Being blind gave me a whole new life. I didn't ask for it." She licked the grease from her fingers. "That's why I'd rather talk to someone on the phone or computer. Because then we're the same. We're equals."

"What do you mean, equals?"

Cheyenne tried to put into words what she had never

before said out loud. "Think about how much of talking has to do with what you see and not what you hear. When you meet new people, you can tell a lot about them even before they've opened their mouth. Just by their clothes, how they stand, the expression on their face. But I don't see any of that stuff anymore. Plus, in real life I'm always talking to people who have already walked away, or I answer people who aren't really talking to me. But when I talk to someone on the computer or the phone, we're at the same level. We know exactly the same amount of information."

While she spoke, Cheyenne slipped her hand into her coat pocket and felt the piece of glass nestled in the kibble. It reassured her a bit. The glass was like a secret weapon. She ran her finger lightly along one edge, even as she spoke without a pause. She knew Griffin had no idea what she was doing. Sighted people always had to look, even at things their fingers were already telling them about. They couldn't find what was in their pockets without looking down, couldn't hunt through a purse without sticking their head inside. She knew because she had once been one of them.

But blind people knew how to do things without giving themselves away. Their hands could work in the dark, like moles, blindly tunneling but always getting where they needed to go. Blind people could look like they were paying attention to you when they were really paying attention to something else.

"What happened, anyway? Your dad said you were in an accident."

The silence stretched out before Cheyenne finally found herself answering him. "It was the summer I was thirteen. My mom grew up in Medford, and we were down there visiting my grandmother. Just the two of us. My dad was on a business trip. Because of Nike, he travels a lot." She took a deep breath. "We had gone for a long walk, and the sun had just set. It was me, my mom, and my dog, Spencer. We were facing traffic, walking down this long, straight road without any sidewalks, just gravel on the side of the road. Each car that came up behind us would throw our shadows way ahead of us, so they were as long as the block and really thin." As she spoke, she saw it with her mind's eye. "Then as each car got closer, our shadows got closer and closer and shorter and shorter. I told my mom it looked like our shadows were walking backward. That was the last thing I ever said to her."

She remembered how her mom had smiled in the half light, her curls wild as they often were by the end of the day. Her mom had been beautiful, at least that's how Cheyenne remembered it. Her mom didn't spend nearly as much time at the hair stylist or the gym as Danielle did. But she did have plenty of time for Cheyenne. They had laughed at the same jokes, jokes her dad never thought were all that funny. Every Saturday, her mom had taken her to the library and they had each come home with a big stack of books.

When anybody asked Cheyenne what had happened to her, she always just said "car accident" in a tone that made it clear she didn't want to say one more word about it. She never talked about it. Never.

Now she took a shuddery breath. "One minute we were walking, watching our shadows come back to us. The next minute, two cars were coming up behind us. It was two kids racing, so one was in the wrong lane, the lane closest to us. Then that guy saw the headlights of a car coming toward him and panicked. He swerved and hit us." She didn't say that her mom's body had ended up almost a block from where they were first hit.

"The car ran right over Spencer. That was my dog. It didn't hit me full on, or I'd be dead, too. Instead it threw me into a speed limit sign. The top of my head smacked into the pole." Cheyenne realized she was unconsciously pushing her fingers through her bangs, which she always carefully fluffed so that the scar wouldn't show. Her index finger traced the twists of its raised edges. "And my brain got bounced off the back of my skull, and when that happened, it killed the part that tells me what I'm seeing. So my eyes still work. My brain just can't understand the message."

There was a long silence. Then Griffin asked softly, "Were you knocked unconscious?"

"Only for a few seconds. When I woke up, I couldn't see anything. I could feel the blood running down my face, and I told myself that was why I couldn't see. I knew my arm was broken, but everything else seemed to be okay. I was screaming for my mom, feeling around with my good arm. All I could find was one of her shoes. I guess she was literally knocked out of them." Cheyenne fell silent, her head crowded with memories.

Big Words Scare Me

Griffin couldn't sleep. The floor was hard, and the cold seeped up through the old sleeping bag. Exhausted, Cheyenne had dozed off after dinner. Griffin had pulled the quilt over her and then hadn't known what to do with himself. By that time, his dad had been singing along with the stereo, but Griffin knew that when Roy drank, his mood could turn on a dime. Griffin stayed in his bedroom, sitting on the far edge of the bed, alternately looking at comic books and watching Cheyenne, until finally his dad had turned off the music and staggered to bed.

Griffin hadn't known where to sleep. He had thought about sleeping on the couch, but he didn't want to leave Cheyenne alone. Partly he wanted to watch her; partly he wanted to watch over her. He had finally settled for the floor. Now he regretted his decision. Cheyenne's sleep had turned restless, making it even harder for him to doze off. She kept moaning and kicking her feet.

Finally he sat up and looked at her. He could make out the dark tangle of her hair, but that was about it. She sounded like she had gotten sicker, but in the dark, it was hard to judge just how sick she really was. Then Griffin realized that the normal rules didn't apply. Moving quietly, he got up and flicked on the light, wincing at the sudden brightness.

Cheyenne didn't stir. She lay curled on her side. He knelt down next to the bed so he could look at her more closely. Her mouth was full and soft, the lips slightly parted. When she exhaled, her breath rattled in her chest. Black strands of damp hair clung to her flushed face. It looked like she had a fever.

Griffin's hand hovered over her forehead, then gently pressed down. Her expression didn't change. She seemed hot—but how hot, exactly? If your fever got too high, couldn't it damage your brain?

Griffin put his free hand on his own forehead. That felt hot, too. He tried moving his right hand from Cheyenne's forehead to his own, but he couldn't really feel any difference, except that hers was clammy and his wasn't. Obviously his palm was useless as a thermometer. Then he had an idea. If he touched his forehead to hers, he would be able to tell for sure how much warmer she was.

Griffin leaned forward and tentatively pressed his forehead against Cheyenne's. Definitely warmer. Was her brain cooking inside her skull? While he was still wondering if he should just try to sneak her out of the house and dump her outside a hospital, Cheyenne sat up with a jerk. Their heads cracked together.

She yelped and pushed him away.

"Shh!" He didn't want her to wake Roy. "It's just me. Griffin."

Cheyenne dropped her own voice to a whisper. "What are you doing?" She sounded clearer than he thought he would in similar circumstances. "Are you trying to kiss me or something?"

"No!" To his embarrassment, his voice broke. "I was just trying to figure out if you had a fever."

"And?"

"And I think you do."

"I know *that*." She sat up, scooted back until her shoulders were against the wall, folded her arms, and rested them on top of her knees. She still wore her striped scarf and the puffy silver coat.

Griffin persisted. "But I think you're sicker than you were." He thought of what her father had said on the radio. Cheyenne couldn't really *die* from pneumonia, could she? Although didn't people used to die from pneumonia, back in the old days, before there were antibiotics?

They must have been thinking along the same lines, because Cheyenne said, "The doctor said that pneumonia used to be called the old man's friend. Because that's what a lot of people died from when they were old and frail."

"Some friend," Griffin said, then added, "Wait a second. I have an idea."

He tiptoed down the hall and into the bathroom. The shower curtain still lay in the bottom of the tub. *Crap.* He had forgotten about that. Cheyenne's escape attempt seemed like it had happened in another lifetime. He tried to hang the curtain back up, wincing as it rattled, but it had ripped away from the rings. When Roy asked, Griffin was going to have to say that he had tripped and fallen—or maybe, Griffin realized, that Cheyenne had. That was more believable.

He let the curtain fall back into the tub, then knelt and opened up the cupboard beneath the sink. Under the silver curve of pipe, a blue plastic basket held rubbing alcohol, Advil, a broken comb, and stray Band-Aids. No thermometer. But mixed in were all kinds of medicines that, for one reason or another, had never been used or used up. Griffin pawed through muscle relaxants, rash creams, and cough suppressants. He scooped up the Advil and cough medicine. Then after holding up amber bottle after amber bottle to the light, he finally saw, with a surge of triumph, the word Cipro. He knew that Cipro was an antibiotic. The printed label read "Janie Sawyer."

It was kind of a surprise to see his mom's name. He had a sudden flash of memory—her dark eyes, her high cheekbones, the long reddish-brown hair that fell to her waist. She had hidden behind that hair when she was angry or sad or any of a dozen emotions that Roy didn't want to hear about. Sometimes she had stood up to Roy, but not very often. And Roy had only gotten worse after she left.

According to the label on the bottle, the prescription had expired six and a half years ago; one year to the day after his mom had filled it. But what were the chances that a medicine suddenly gave up the ghost exactly 365 days later? They probably had to put that date on for legal reasons. Or to give them an excuse to sell you some more. Griffin opened the bottle. The white capsules looked okay. He sniffed. They didn't smell like anything in particular.

The directions said you were supposed to take one pill three times a day for seven days. There weren't that many pills left—maybe eight or nine—but it would be enough to give Cheyenne a start.

In the kitchen, he filled one of the glasses he had washed earlier. Back in his bedroom, he softly closed the door behind him and then said in a half whisper, "Since you can't go pick up your prescription, I thought the prescription should come to you."

Cheyenne looked confused. "What?"

"Cipro." Griffin rattled the bottle. When she still looked blank, he added, "It's an antibiotic."

"But don't they use different kinds of antibiotics depending on what you're sick with? What if this one doesn't work for pneumonia?"

"I don't see how you would be any worse off." Why

didn't she appreciate the effort he was making? "Look, it probably can't hurt and it might help."

"But what if it only half kills the pneumonia bacteria and the rest of them come back stronger? We've been learning about antibiotic resistance in biology."

Griffin sighed and sat down on the bed. "What is it with you? Does everything have to be an argument or a discussion?"

She answered him seriously. "Yes. Yes, it does." Her roughened voice made her sound older.

"Well, take one anyway. Plus, I've got Advil for your fever and medicine for your cough." He pressed the pills into one hand and the glass into the other. Would it help if she doubled up the number of antibiotics? He realized he could tell her the package said whatever he wanted—that she was to take them ten times a day with wine, or once every two weeks, even that they were some different drug entirely.

Instead he said, "Where are you taking biology? Are you going to a special school for blind people?"

Cheyenne shook her head. "I'm mainstreamed. I go to Catlin Gabel."

Griffin snorted. "Mainstreamed! Even I know that's a fancy-pants private school."

Cheyenne flushed. "Well, it's not some special school for the handicapped, anyway. I'm the only blind person there, which can be kind of hard. Sometimes teachers forget and point at things or write stuff on the board and don't say what they've written. It doesn't happen so much now that I've got Phantom. It's like he's a visual cue. 'Oh, right, Cheyenne's blind.' " She put the pills in her mouth, took a sip of water, and tipped her head back. He watched her throat move up and down.

"What other classes are you taking besides biology?"

She set the glass on the dresser and rubbed her face. "Advanced placement history, German, junior-level English, and trig."

"Oh," Griffin said. He felt stupid, the way he used to feel when he still went to school.

She didn't seem to notice. "Since I'm blind, I have to take extra classes. I have a computer class in a special room they set up for me. The computers at school and at home have a program that can read to me, although sometimes it pronounces things wrong and the voice is really flat." Cheyenne said the next few words like a robot. "And it reads every word I type so I know right away if I make a mistake."

"What about the reading assignments? Do you have a machine that reads books to you?"

"Reading." Cheyenne let out a long sigh. "I miss reading, you know, just picking up a book. There's a million ways to read if you're blind, but none of them are as good. Sometimes Danielle pays someone to read to me. And volunteers read my textbooks. With one of them, it's some guy who always sounds like he has a cold—*wid a code*. It's nearly impossible to make out what he's saying. That's why I like CDs and downloads so much better, you know, like Books on Tape, the same as sighted people buy. Have you ever heard the guy who reads Harry Potter?" Her face lit up. "He's wonderful. He has a different voice for every character."

Griffin smiled back at her. Cheyenne was smiling, too, but of course it wasn't a shared smile. It must be weird not to be able to have a nonverbal conversation just by rolling your eyes at someone, or grinning, or stifling a yawn.

"But when I read on my own," Cheyenne continued, "I'm not a very good reader."

Griffin was surprised. "Really? But you're smart."

"I mean, I'm not that good at Braille."

"Braille's like those little dots on the elevator buttons, right?"

She nodded. "Yeah. You feel the different dots in each Braille cell. You have to memorize what each of them means. I have friends who were born blind, and they're a lot faster than me. They can even use both hands to read. I can't do that. I have to go really slow, and even then I get confused. If I get one dot wrong, then it could mean an entirely different word. Big words scare me."

Cheyenne had no idea how well Griffin understood her. "But you would know big words if someone said them to you, right?"

"Of course. I just can't read them."

"I have a hard time reading, too," he admitted. "Last year, I had to read aloud in class. And there was this word, and I kept saying it 'Brie. Fly. Brie-fly.' It was supposed to be an article about flowers, but all I could think about was a piece of cheese with a fly on it."

"Brie-fly," Cheyenne said, echoing the way he had said it, before she got it right. "Oh. Briefly. It makes sense. Have you ever been tested for dyslexia?"

"I'm not retarded," Griffin said quickly, wishing that he hadn't opened up to her.

"No, that's not what being dyslexic means. Dyslexia is having trouble with the physical part of reading, not the comprehension part. Like me having trouble with Braille." She straightened up. "You could get tapes from the same place I do. They're not only for blind people. You just order them through the school district."

"What makes you think I'm still going to school?" Griffin said, feeling deflated. He had been hoping she thought he was about thirty. Thirty seemed like a good age.

"You live with your dad, for one thing." Cheyenne shrugged. "I don't know. The more I listened to you, the more I figured you were about my age. Blind people are good at sizing other people up." She leaned forward. "That's why I know you're not like the other guys here."

Nothing but Ifs

Cheyenne could do the math. These men thought they could get five million dollars from her dad. And they probably could, if he had enough time. And after that they would have two choices.

Choice one: Free the girl who could help the police find them.

Choice two: Kill the girl and find a good place to hide her body.

And the longer she was here, the more they might start thinking that it wasn't in their best interests to pick the first choice. Because, blind or not, she would know too much.

Forcing herself to take a deep breath, Cheyenne tried to calm down. These guys were criminals, yes, but they were car thieves, not killers. And that was a pretty big difference. Griffin had kidnapped her only by accident. And while it was true that he could go to jail for that, maybe his sentence wouldn't be too bad because he hadn't meant to do it. But murder—she forced herself to think of what she really meant—actually killing her, for that they could be put to death themselves. That had to serve as a deterrent. Didn't it?

But then Cheyenne thought of how empty the roads had been on the way here, and the impression of stillness and space that had surrounded them as they walked to the house. Even though the punishment for murder was much worse than it was for kidnapping, that still assumed someone would find her body.

Her head felt muddled and thick, but she forced herself to think straight. Just by the way the three older men treated her, she could tell that they saw her as a thing, not a person. They probably saw everyone as things, but her blindness just made it easier for them to write her off.

Griffin was the only one who might want to save her. Cheyenne had to make sure he continued to see her as a person. She had to make him care about protecting her. She had to give him a reason to hesitate. No more arguing with him, she vowed. No more fighting. Because her life depended on it.

But Cheyenne knew it was a one-way street. If she had a moment when she might turn the tables, she had to be willing to do whatever it took. Even if it meant hurting Griffin. Even if it meant worse than that. Because she was pretty sure this situation was going to end with somebody dead.

After a long pause, Griffin said, "How come you think I'm not like them?" She couldn't read the emotions that colored his voice.

"You're kind, for one thing. And for another, I think you're smarter than they are." Cheyenne was telling the truth. If she had to lie, she hoped she could make that sound like the truth, too.

He shook his head hard enough that she could feel it because the bed wiggled. "I'm not smart. I dropped out of school before they could kick me out."

"I don't believe it. Maybe you have troubles reading, but I do too, and I'm still smart, and so are you. If you start believing what other people think, you'll never get anywhere."

Cheyenne thought of her biology teacher, Mr. Waddell. Even though he insisted his name was wa-DELL, the kids all called him Mr. Waddle. "Just because you have a handicap, I'm not going to be lenient with you," he had informed Cheyenne, asking her to stay behind after her first class with him. "Don't expect any special considerations from me. You will be treated like any other student." Of course, was he really any worse than Ms. Crispin, who taught English? For their project, everyone in the group had gotten a failing grade. Cheyenne got a B. For the exact same project. Two weeks ago, Ms. Crispin had said to Cheyenne, "I wanted to tell you how impressed I am. You can hardly tell you have a handicap."

Griffin's bitter voice snapped Cheyenne back into the

here and now. "You really think it makes any difference what I think of myself? You really think I could be anybody I wanted to, even president of the United States? You've got to face facts, Cheyenne. You're blind, which means you're never going to be able to do a million things. And the facts of my life mean I don't have many choices, either. I don't have many choices at all."

"So does that mean you just have to go along with what's happening here? Just because you took my step-mom's car doesn't mean you have to keep going down this road with them."

"What are you thinking? Are you thinking I'm going to drive you to the police station and turn myself in?"

Put like that, Cheyenne could hear how ridiculous the idea was. But what would happen to her? She blurted out her fear. "I don't think they're ever going to let me go."

"Of course they will." Griffin sounded like he was trying to convince himself.

"You know as well as I do what the easiest solution would be," Cheyenne countered. "For them to keep the money and get rid of me. I'm the only witness. Probably nobody saw you at the shopping mall. Certainly not well enough to recognize you. And it was a fluke thing. You have no connection to my family or to me. None. Mean-while, the police will be looking at people connected to Catlin Gabel, and every housekeeper and groundskeeper we've ever had, *and* people Dad knows through Nike.

They'll look at everyone who works at Nike now or who has ever worked there, including all the people who have been fired from Nike and all the people who hate Nike because they think it has overseas sweatshops."

"That's a pretty big list. That's practically the United States of America."

"Right," Cheyenne said. "So what are the chances that they'll find you guys? Probably pretty slim. Unless you give me back. And those other guys won't believe me if I say I won't tell. That if you let me go, I won't say anything. But I promise I won't."

"We're gonna give you back, okay? We'll take you someplace safe and turn you loose." Griffin sounded as if he wished he believed what he was saying.

There had to be a way for her to get out of this alive, Cheyenne thought. There had to.

"What would have happened if I had gone through the bathroom window? What's back there, anyway?"

"Nothing. No people anyway, at least not for most of it. It's just woods. It stretches on for miles. To the east, there's a river. To the west, there's our road, and after about four miles, that meets up with a bigger road. But it's still pretty quiet. You probably would have just wandered around and got lost and died. It gets down pretty far below freezing at night."

Cheyenne opened her mouth to say something but found herself yawning so she made a creaking noise.

She felt his cool hand on her forehead. "I think the Advil brought your fever down. You need to get to sleep. We both do." He pulled the blanket up to her chin. "The floor's too hard. I'm going to sleep on the other side of the bed in a sleeping bag. Don't worry—I won't bother you or anything."

Cheyenne knew that if she could see, Griffin's face would be bright red.

She heard him stand up, turn off the light, then felt him sit on the other side of the bed. Rustling as he got into his sleeping bag. No part of him touched her, so she knew he must be lying just on the edge of the bed.

She was exhausted, but she was also wide awake. She couldn't pin her hopes on Griffin. He might stop things from happening, but he probably wouldn't. After all, he was just a kid. Like her.

Long after Griffin's breathing had reached an even rhythm, Cheyenne lay awake, trying to think of a way out.

If she could get to a phone.

If she could find another way to alert the authorities.

If she could persuade Griffin to save her.

If she could escape.

Nothing but ifs.

Let's Send Him a Finger

When Griffin woke up, he didn't know where he was. He was on the wrong side of the bed, in a sleeping bag, with someone breathing right next to him.

And then it all came back to him in a rush.

He levered himself on one elbow. Cheyenne's breathing hitched, but then straightened out again. Her face was still pale, except for the flush across her cheeks, but she didn't look as bad as she had the night before. He wondered if this was how married people felt when one of them woke up and the other one was still asleep. Her mouth was soft and vulnerable. Underneath her pale lids, her eyes moved back and forth. What was she seeing in her dreams?

Even though he had gotten just a few hours of sleep, Griffin was now wide awake. He managed to get off the bed with a minimum of rustling. He padded out into the kitchen, the floor icy under his bare feet. The woodstove was going in the living room, but the heat only went so far.

Griffin was surprised to find Roy, awake, leaning against the counter, drinking coffee. Next to him, the phone lay on the counter. Or what was left of the phone. Someone had taken a hammer to it. Now it was shards of plastic and colorful wires. Griffin was surprised he hadn't heard his dad whaling on it the night before. He poked at it.

"What happened to the phone?"

Roy shrugged. "Insurance. I don't want her getting loose and calling anyone. Now she can't." His eyes were bloodshot and his hands shaky.

Griffin wondered why his dad hadn't just unplugged it and stuck it on a high shelf, but there was no use asking. "What if I need to call someone?"

"You can use that cell I got." He looked over Griffin's shoulder. "Is she sleeping?"

"Yeah. In the middle of the night, she seemed like she was running a fever. I went through the stuff in the bathroom and found an old prescription of Mom's to give her."

At the mention of the bathroom, Griffin had been sure his dad would remember to ask what had happened to the shower curtain. Instead, he just looked startled. "Your mom's? Really?"

His dad never talked about his mom anymore. But after Griffin came home from the hospital, he would sometimes find his dad crying and holding something that used to belong to his mom—a bracelet or a sweater. She had left a lot of stuff behind. They had had a big fight about what had happened to Griffin. It must have been the last straw, because she had taken off with her purse and her car and some pictures of Griffin and that was it. Gone so good that she never looked back.

"Mom had the prescription filled a few months before she left, but she only took about half the pills."

Roy nodded and lifted the cup of coffee to his lips. Griffin couldn't read the expression on his face.

They heard the front door open and then the sounds of TJ and Jimbo coming in.

"What's the word?" Jimbo asked when he walked into the kitchen. Today he was wearing an extra-long stocking cap and padded ski pants. "Have you talked to them?"

"I got off the phone with the dad about twenty minutes ago. He says they can't raise that kind of money. Not in cash. Not that fast."

"I'll bet we can speed things up," Jimbo said. "Let's send him a finger."

Griffin couldn't tell if he was joking.

"Or an ear," TJ added. He definitely wasn't joking.

To Griffin's intense relief, Roy shook his head. "We do that and they'll decide she might be dead already and hunt us down with guns blazing. We start chopping off body parts and they'll figure they've got nothing left to lose."

"Did they say how much they could give us?" Griffin asked. He kept his voice soft, hoping to influence the others to talk more quietly. He couldn't imagine what it would be like for Cheyenne if she woke up and heard them talking about lopping off her fingers or ears.

"A million." Setting down his coffee cup, Roy scrubbed his face with open palms. "I told him I would call him back." His voice was glum, even though a few days ago he would have been over the moon about the prospect of getting a million dollars.

"That's still a lot," Griffin said. "That's like $250,000 apiece."

Roy shook his head. "You're still a minor, and you still live under my roof. I'm going to watch after your share."

TJ and Jimbo exchanged a look. "Do you really think that's fair?" Jimbo asked. "You get a cool half million, and we get only half of that?"

Roy straightened up, and Jimbo and TJ automatically took a step back.

"Hey, I'm the one who is taking all the risks here. She's on my property, and it's my voice that's getting tape-recorded every time I call. And I'm the one figuring out the logistics."

"Logistics?" TJ echoed. It was clear the word wasn't quite familiar.

"The plans. When I call back, I'll tell the dad to be ready to make the drop at three this morning. Then, at three, I'll tell him to drive someplace. But when he gets there, we'll tell him to take another phone we'll have waiting and ditch his first one. I'll have one of you there watching to make sure he does leave his phone. The new phone will have outgoing calls disabled. So he won't be able to tip anyone off. And then I'll call him on the new phone and tell him to make the drop at Ironwood Road." Ironwood Road was a long stretch that linked together two other equally desolate roads. It was quiet no matter what time of the day or night it was. At three in the morning in the middle of winter, it would be dead. "And I'll have one of you watching Ironwood Road before he even knows that's the drop site. Then we'll grab the money and leave the bag in case they put something in it, like a tracer or those exploding dye packs they use on bank robbers. Then we'll come back here and split up the money and go our separate ways."

Jimbo let out a whistle. "Sounds slick."

Griffin didn't care about the money. The idea of it didn't even seem real. "After we get the money, then what?"

"I think we should all get out of town," Roy said. "I know I am. I'm headed down to the airport to get on the first flight I can find to someplace warm where they put an umbrella in your drink."

"Wait, we won't be working here no more?" TJ looked confused.

"You won't need to work, dummy." Jimbo shook his head. "That's the whole point. You won't need to work for years and years. If we go down to someplace where they don't ever see tourists and haven't jacked up their prices, we'll never run out of money."

Griffin couldn't believe they seemed to have forgotten the girl who was in the middle of all this. "But what about Cheyenne?"

Roy's face twisted. "What about her?"

"We'll let her go, right? We've never used our names. And of course she has no idea what we look like." Griffin made his voice as certain as he could. Hearing Cheyenne say, "I know your name. It's Griffin. And now I know for sure your dad's name is Roy. When I tell the police that, they'll find you in a minute." Griffin didn't know how to make things right. He just knew that he couldn't stand by and let something bad happen to Cheyenne.

Roy looked skeptical. "Sooner or later, she'll tell them something that will let them know exactly where we are."

Griffin remembered his earlier conversation with Cheyenne. "Not if we're careful, she won't. For one thing, she's the daughter of Nike's president. Do you know how many people would want a piece of that pie? When you call back, you can say something to make them think it's all about Nike. They'll spend years tracking down every person who's protested against them or worked there. And they'll never find us. Because they won't realize it was random. That it didn't have anything to do with Nike at all."

Roy thought about this for a while. The other three were silent, watching him.

"On the way to the airport we can slip up into Washington and drop her off along a logging road or something,"

Griffin said. "Point her in the right direction and tell her to start walking. And by the time somebody finds her, we'll be on the beach. With our mai tais."

"Of course," Roy said. Griffin was pretty sure Roy had never said "of course" before in his life.

At least not when he meant it.

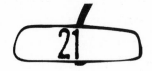

Intelligent Disobedience

For a few minutes after she woke up, Cheyenne didn't know where she was. And then she remembered. And wished she hadn't.

By the sliver of light she could see with her left eye, Cheyenne decided that it was morning. Real light was warmer, somehow, than light that came from a bulb. But when she felt her watch, she was surprised to find it was one twenty. So afternoon, not morning. Then someone opened the bedroom door. Cheyenne braced herself.

"Are you awake?" When she heard Griffin's voice, relief flooded through her.

"Yeah." She pushed herself up until her back was against the wall.

"I brought you some Advil to keep your fever down and another one of those antibiotics. Plus OJ to wash it down with and some crackers. I'll put the crackers at nine o'clock."

She felt him settle on the bed by her feet, and then he put the glass in one hand and the pills in the other.

"Thanks," she said, trying to sound like she meant it. "When am I going home?"

"Soon. My dad's just making the final arrangements. There's going to be a drop tonight at three, and then we'll drive you someplace and let you go." His voice changed to a whisper, and he leaned close enough that she could feel his breath stir her hair. "The thing is, you can't let on that you know my name or my dad's name. You have to act like you don't know anything."

Cheyenne nodded, biting her lip.

Griffin's soft whisper continued. "You know how you told me about how many enemies your dad must have? They'll probably say some stuff to try to make you think that you being kidnapped is connected to Nike. Pretend like you believe them."

Cheyenne didn't know who to believe. "Griffin, you've got to promise that they will let me go. Promise me."

He was quiet for a long time. Finally he whispered, "I promise."

Cheyenne started shivering, and it wasn't just from being sick. She was afraid that Griffin's hesitation had said more than his words.

In a more normal voice, he asked, "So how do you get to school? In a limo?"

"Are you kidding? Danielle usually takes me. My dad

might make a lot of money, but he doesn't flaunt it. He's not one of those gross balding guys who drives a Hummer so he can feel more like a real man." She decided not to mention the housekeeper and the cook. She wanted Griffin to continue to think they had things in common.

"On TV, your dad said you have a guide dog. Do you use your dog or a cane to get places?"

The thought of Phantom and her ruined cane made Cheyenne's head feel liquid again. She wouldn't cry. "Mostly I take Phantom, but I took my cane yesterday because my stepmom thought it would be easier."

"Is it weird being towed around by a dog? Can you really trust it?" From the way he said it, Cheyenne wondered how many things Griffin trusted.

"I've only had Phantom three months, but it feels like forever. I wish it *had* been forever, but you can't get a guide dog until you're sixteen." She thought of how she had woken the first morning after she got Phantom to find his head draped across her neck. At that moment, Cheyenne had known they belonged together. "And I totally trust him. He watches out for anything that might hurt me—curbs, low-hanging branches, skateboarders, telephone poles, holes in the sidewalk. Once he even saved my life."

Griffin touched her knee. "What happened?"

"I was crossing at an intersection when this car turned right without even stopping. Phantom threw himself against my legs and pushed me until I stepped back." Cheyenne remembered the screech of skidding tires, the rush of air as a car whizzed by so close that the fender must have ruffled Phantom's fur. Other drivers had honked and yelled, but the car never stopped. "If Phantom hadn't pushed me out of the way, we would both probably have been killed. And if I had just had my cane, I definitely would have been killed."

"So using a dog is better than using a cane?"

"*Everything* is better with a guide dog. The difference between having a dog and a cane is astronomical. Before, it was like I was invisible. Now people *talk* to me. They tell me how smart Phantom is, even if he's just lying down. They tell me stories about their dogs. They want to pet him. Sometimes I have to be kind of snippy, you know, 'My dog is working.' But the biggest difference is just in getting around. Now I zip through people and it's smooth. Phantom is so good that I can walk down the hall at school and never even rub shoulders with anyone else."

When Cheyenne had first gone back to school, with only her cane to guide her, it had been so hard. Except for Kenzie and Sadie, most of her friends had hung back as if Cheyenne was a different person, someone they didn't even know.

The thing was, they were right. Before the accident, Cheyenne had been outgoing. She sang to herself, chattered, laughed, called out to everyone she saw in the halls.

After the accident, she quieted down. It was more than just sadness. Without her sight, her ears were her connection to other human beings. Blindness took away the nonverbal cues that let her know whether someone else was tired, sad, happy, or worried. If she listened closely, she could still pick these emotions up in voices. But as a result, her own voice was muted.

The rehab center had corridors just wide enough for two people to pass each other. At Catlin Gabel, the walls seemed like they were miles apart. If it was crowded, she was forced to walk in the middle of the hall, without the security of a wall. The worst part were the breaks between classes, when she had only a few minutes to get to the next room. If she was hurrying and ran into someone, it embarrassed them, which meant it totally embarrassed Cheyenne.

Then once she was in the right classroom—and before she got Phantom, she could never be completely sure that she was—she had to find her chair with a minimum of bumping. Wondering who the boys were on either side. Who was watching her. If they were laughing. She wanted to be cool and graceful, but instead she felt clumsy and sweaty. Now with Phantom, Cheyenne walked with poise and speed. He had returned her body to her.

Just thinking about Phantom made Cheyenne's eyes sting with tears. She loved the soft fur of his ears, his long, slender muzzle, even the sound of his toenails on the floor. Phantom tried to keep quiet when he was getting into mischief, because he had figured out that Cheyenne couldn't see him. When he was thirsty, he scraped his bowl along the floor to let her know. When he wanted a treat, he barked and put his paws on the counter. And when he was tired, he curled up under Cheyenne's desk or inside the empty fireplace, even in the shower stall.

Cheyenne hoped it wasn't really obvious that she was crying again. At the same time, she didn't want to stop talking, not when Griffin seemed interested. She wanted to bind him to her with gauzy ropes of words. She took a deep breath and said, "But a dog's not just a machine. You don't work your dog when you're at home. A dog needs time to just be a dog. How about that dog you've got outside? When is it ever just a dog?"

"Duke?" Griffin let out a surprised laugh. "Duke's not a dog. Not really." He snorted again, as if the idea was ridiculous. Then he asked, "So how does your dog know where to take you?"

Cheyenne shook her head. "He doesn't. It's not like Phantom's a cab driver. I can't say 'McDonald's, please' and have him take me there. I do half the work. I need to have a map inside my head of all the streets we'll cross and tell him when to make all the turns. When I get to an intersection, I'm the one who has to decide whether the light is red or green just by listening. To a dog, red, green, and yellow look the same. Then when I reach the right block, I have to listen or feel for clues to help me find the building

I want. I'm the navigator. Phantom is the one who makes sure I can walk there without running into anything or being run over."

"Wait—you just get to a street and then listen to see if the cars are stopped? That sounds kind of dangerous. What happens if you tell Phantom to go but a car's coming?"

"Your dog is trained to judge whether your command is safe," Cheyenne said. "It's called intelligent disobedience."

A Big Mistake

"Intelligent disobedience, huh?" Griffin echoed. He liked the way it sounded. Whenever he didn't do what somebody wanted, they always assumed he was making a big mistake.

"What's funny is that when Phantom doesn't do something I tell him to, I still get annoyed," Cheyenne said, "like he's being stupid. And then I figure out that he's right." She drank her orange juice in one long gulp and then wiped the back of her mouth with her hand. She had already gobbled the crackers.

Belatedly, Griffin realized she must be hungry. "Would you like some lunch?"

She nodded. "Sure. That would be great."

"I'll go see what I can find." He got up, already mentally rummaging through the kitchen. There was some ramen in the cupboard and maybe some peas in the freezer. And he could cut up some hot dogs and put them in, too.

He would break up the noodles so they wouldn't be too messy when Cheyenne ate them. He thought he would tell her how ramen was kind of like stone soup, because it was only good when you added a bunch of stuff to it. And maybe she would laugh, or at least smile.

While Griffin was digging through the fridge, looking for eggs, TJ came in. "You making something to eat?"

"For our guest."

"Got enough for TJ?"

Griffin didn't like to say yes about anything to TJ, but he couldn't think of a good reason to say no. He nodded. As TJ went down the hall to the bathroom, Griffin took the pan off the heat and added more water so that the food would stretch further. It was only as he was slicing the hot dogs over the pan that his brain translated the sounds he had heard. It hadn't been the door to the bathroom that had opened. It had been the door to his own bedroom.

TJ was alone with Cheyenne.

Griffin dropped the hot dog as well as the knife, although later he thought about how he should have taken it. He ran down the hall and flung open the bedroom door.

TJ was leaning over Cheyenne. Her back was against the wall, her knees drawn up against her chest, making a barrier between them. Her eyes were narrowed in concentration, and her lips were pulled back from her teeth, like a dog silently snarling. TJ had one knee on the bed and both of her wrists in one fist, pinioning her to the wall. And he was trying to take off Cheyenne's coat with the other hand.

With a roar, Griffin launched himself forward. His fist landed on the side of TJ's head.

TJ fell on the bed and rolled over on his back, howling. His cap had fallen off and slid down his skinny ponytail.

"What the hell do you think you're doing, TJ?" Griffin shouted. He had been afraid of what TJ would do to Cheyenne, but he wasn't as worried about what TJ would do to him. TJ always knew when to put his tail between his legs. And right now, Griffin was ready to kill him.

Cheyenne scrambled off the bed. She tried to run for the door and fell when the cord around her ankle yanked her back.

Griffin leaned down to help her up, and she clawed him. "It's me," he said, but Cheyenne still pushed him away and then got to her feet without anyone's assistance. She squeezed herself between the bed and the desk until her back was against the wall. She was panting, but she wasn't crying. Griffin suddenly thought that if he had brought the knife into the room, Cheyenne would have sunk it into both of them, in turn. Without a second thought.

"Just what do you think you're doing?"

"Look at her, all shiny," TJ whined. "I just wanted to take a little bit of the shine off. It's just like Jimbo says. She's so rich she probably wipes her ass with twenty-dollar bills. She probably thinks her crap doesn't even smell. I was just going to teach her a little lesson. Make her understand how the other half lives."

TJ was saying all this with snot running out of his nose. Griffin's hands were clenched into fists. He wanted to hit TJ again so bad. "Say that again. What did Jimbo say?"

Something like hope played across TJ's face. He half sat up. "Oh, you know, he was going on about how she probably thinks she's too good for us. And that she needed to be taken down a notch."

"And you listened to that BS?" Griffin rubbed his fist. His middle knuckle was swelling. "Get out. Before I change my mind."

After TJ scuttled out carrying his hat, Griffin locked the door behind him. He pressed the button more for Cheyenne's benefit than anything else. He walked back and stood in front of her. She was trembling.

"It's okay. He's gone. I'm sorry I left you alone. I won't let that happen again." With the tip of his index finger, he touched her cheekbone. "I'm sorry."

Her shaking intensified, and he was afraid he had frightened her all the more. But when he tentatively reached out his arms, she put her face against his chest. Her breath smelled like orange juice. He held her tight and rocked her back and forth. It reminded Griffin of the one school dance he had gone to, when slow dancing just meant shuffling your feet.

Just as he was getting used to the feel of her in his arms,

Cheyenne stepped back. She pulled her coat into place. "He was going to hurt me. Rape me, maybe kill me. And I think he would have, too, if you hadn't come in. What kind of person could feel like I deserved that?"

Griffin sighed. "Jimbo got him riled up. He likes to wind TJ up and watch where he goes. Out in the real world, nobody pays them any attention. To them, rich people aren't real. They're people in magazines and TV. Those two aren't around rich people very much." He let out a little self-conscious laugh. "Of course, I'm not either. But just like rich people would probably look at us and see white trash, those two don't think rich people are human either."

Cheyenne's next words were a surprise. "What happened to your throat? The skin felt different there."

Griffin kept his answer short, letting his tone make it clear that he didn't want to talk about it. "It got burned."

"How?" It was like she wanted to make him feel as vulnerable as she did.

"In an accident."

"What kind of accident?"

"My dad was cooking, all right?"

"Cooking?" He could hear the disbelief in her voice. Even Cheyenne had figured out that Roy would never cook anything.

"My dad was making some meth, and a little of it spilled on a burner."

"Meth?" She didn't seem sure about what it was.

Griffin envied her innocence. "Crystal, Tina, crank, ice. Basically, it's speed. Amphetamines. You used to be able to make it with stuff you could get at the grocery store. That's how my dad made extra money before they started locking up some of the ingredients. Then he lost his job and switched to stealing cars."

"So to make it, you have to cook it?"

"Yeah. It smells terrible. Like cat piss. I went out to the barn to ask him something and then, when it flared up, I got burned on my throat and chest."

Griffin remembered how at first it had felt either really, really hot or really, really cold. He hadn't been able to tell which, and then suddenly it was hot, red hot, eating through him. He managed to rip off his shirt or he would have been burned even worse. The pain had been so great he had wanted to die or pass out. After a few seconds, he narrowed his choices down to just one: He wanted to die.

He did neither.

It was his mom who took him to the emergency room, his mom who made up some story about the woodstove. The doctors asked her to leave the room and then questioned Griffin about it again. He knew they didn't believe her.

Griffin stuck to the same story. Not out of love for Roy, but because he was afraid his mom would get in trouble, too.

He had spent a month in the burn unit. IVs in the backs

of both hands and a tube in his throat to help him breathe because the mucous lining had been burned, too. Even with the tube down his throat, he had still been able to smell. The burn unit had been full of smells. The strongest came from the Silvadene salve, which was the color and consistency of Crisco and smelled like peppermint. Twice a day, the nurses spread it over his oozing burns. And underneath the Silvadene was another stench, sweet and rotten.

Every night Griffin lay in the dark and listened to monitors beeping, ventilators whooshing, machines monitoring the thin threads of life. He heard other patients pleading, praying, screaming. Most of them frightened him. One was a homeless man who had been set on fire by bored teens. Another was a boy only a few years older than Griffin who had tried to kill himself by soaking his clothes with gasoline and lighting a match. And there was a little kid, two or three years old, who had tugged on the cord of a deep-fat fryer and pulled it over on himself. One woman had been burned in a car accident. She had died on the third day he was there.

In Griffin's nightmares, the nurses in their blue plastic gowns, rubber gloves, and paper bonnets were again wheeling him to the debridement room to scrub off his dead flesh with wire-bristled brushes.

Even after his burns healed, he was reminded of them constantly. Every morning, his fingers traced the red, hairless scars when he soaped his chest and neck in the shower, or touched the shallower scars on the insides of his thighs where they had taken the skin grafts. Strangers stared at the shine of tight skin on his throat. Every touch, every stare, brought it all back: the lights, the screams, the whispers, the smells.

When he was out of the house, he wore his shirts buttoned up to the neck, but people still noticed the scars. His shirt collar didn't hide everything, and once people noticed, most of them couldn't stop staring, whether it was in a movie line or at the grocery store. Some looked at him and quickly looked away. Some pretended not to look—and then stared if they thought he hadn't noticed. And a few made a point of meeting his eyes and smiling, like he was some kind of a retard or a dog who might turn on them.

He hated the smiles worst of all.

Every day Griffin was in the hospital, his mother had visited him. And then one day, right before he was released, she didn't come.

"So I've been kind of wondering—where's your mom?" Cheyenne asked. It was spooky, like she could read his mind.

"What do you mean?"

"I mean, you live here with your dad, but you obviously had to have had a mom, so where is she?"

"She and my dad didn't get along," Griffin said shortly. "So she moved back to Chicago. That's where she grew up."

She used to tell him stories about Chicago, about the lake in the summer and the wind in the winter. Roy didn't like to hear them, so she only told them when he wasn't around.

When Roy finally came to visit Griffin in the hospital, he had told Griffin that his mom had left. She had fought with Roy about the drugs, said she had had enough, and she had left. Roy was expressionless when he broke the news.

It wasn't until he got home that Griffin could see that his dad really *had* been experiencing emotions. First anger (there was a great deal of broken furniture and dishes) and then despair (he hadn't cleaned anything up).

Griffin had thrown away the shards, straightened up what was left, and gotten on without speaking about it. Just as he had with his burns. Just as he had when his mother never wrote or called. He had Googled her a few times at school, but the few Janie Sawyers he found were never the right age.

Cheyenne was quiet for a long time. Then she said in a low voice, "Do you think your dad will really let me go?"

"He says he will."

"That's not what I asked."

The truth was that with so much money at stake, Griffin wasn't sure how far he could trust what Roy said. If his dad did let Cheyenne go, if he left the actual doing of it to TJ and Jimbo, Griffin thought now that they might just take her into the woods instead and kill her. Rape her and kill her.

Griffin realized the only one he trusted to let Cheyenne go was himself. He had to do it, even if it meant risking everything. Meant he ended up in prison, along with Roy and TJ and Jimbo. The alternative was Cheyenne being murdered. He couldn't tell her, in case she somehow let it slip to the others. But when everyone was out getting the drop, he would take Cheyenne and go. When there was no chance that one of them would show up at the house and try to stop them. He would put Cheyenne in the truck and drive like hell until he could get someplace with a phone, someplace with nice bright lighting and lots of people. Where even if they caught up with him, TJ and Jimbo might think twice about killing them. And then he would turn her loose and go back and meet his dad and they would go to Mexico or wherever. And he would hope that Cheyenne would keep her promise and not tell the police their names. And hope that the police didn't show up before he could get the hell out of there. Because if they did, they might decide he was one of the bad guys and kill him.

Was he one of the bad guys?

Griffin didn't know anymore.

Time to Act

For the thousandth time, Cheyenne felt the face of her watch, making the tiniest of motions so she wouldn't wake Griffin.

But now the time had finally come. It was two in the morning, the time she had decided to act. The afternoon and evening had dragged by. The three men had stayed in another part of the house, plotting, she presumed, their voices too low for her to hear. Griffin had mostly stayed with her, leaving only to get them something to eat. Cheyenne had catnapped or pretended to. For one thing, she needed to be wide awake when the time came. And the more she slept, the more they would think she was sick and helpless, even though she thought she could feel the antibiotics kicking in. Sleeping, or pretending to, kept her from talking to Griffin. Kept her from thinking that maybe she wouldn't do what she knew she had to.

Miles from here, her father would soon be following instructions to drop off a black duffel bag stuffed tight with money. One that held no tracking devices or dye packs or anything else. Or they would kill her. And her father was to come alone, with no one following him in another car or in the air or even with a computer. Or they would kill her.

Cheyenne knew all this because Roy had made her stand by while he repeated the details. Then he had pressed the phone into her hand long enough for her to choke out "*Daddy, please help me!*" before he snatched it back and pressed the off button.

But it didn't really matter if her father did or did not follow the rules. It didn't matter at all. TJ had told Cheyenne as much when he attacked her. He had climbed on the bed and pinned her wrists against the wall and whispered in her ear.

"Are you a virgin, Cheyenne? Are you? Because maybe it's time for you to become a real woman. Maybe you should let TJ give you a little loving before it's too late."

She had been too frightened to even make a sound. All she had done was shake her head violently. And one of her shakes had connected with TJ's nose.

He had grunted in pain and then his voice became even more oozing and vicious. "Where you're going, you won't be getting any loving. They never talk about getting it on in heaven, do they, baby? Let TJ give you a sweet memory to take to your grave."

Somehow, Cheyenne had mustered enough saliva in her mouth to spit at him. When he muttered a curse, she knew it had met its target. And then Griffin had stormed in and saved her.

But saving her from a would-be rapist was one thing. Stepping in when Roy told TJ or Jimbo to take her for a ride was another. Would he defy these men—including his father—to save her? When saving her would make it much more likely that he would get caught? Wouldn't it simply be easier for Griffin to pretend to himself that they really were going to let her go?

Sure, these men might get caught and go to jail for murder, but they might not. And they were all about short-term thinking. Take TJ. He had wanted to bring her down to his level, so he had groped and pawed at her, not even worrying about Griffin being in the next room.

Cheyenne wished she had been able to reach her pocket before TJ had pinned her to the wall, wished she had used the broken piece of glass on him. She would have liked to have cut his throat. And she could have done it, too.

What she didn't know was whether she could do what needed to be done now.

The men had left several hours earlier, getting into position to make sure that her dad was following the rules. If they were going to come back to the house for something forgotten, they would have done it by now. It was time to act.

Slipping her hand into her pocket, Cheyenne pulled out the piece of glass. Slowly, slowly, she crawled off the end of the bed. Griffin snorted and shifted, but then his breathing resumed a regular rhythm. She slid her feet forward until the cord that bound her ankle was taut as a wire. Bending down, she sawed through it in a few strokes. Her lungs ached, but she was too afraid to breathe except for the tiniest sips. Too afraid she might cough. The slightest sound might give her away.

When the cord parted, it was like taking a step into empty air. There was no turning back. If Griffin woke up, he would have to try to stop her.

Gripping the piece of glass tighter, Cheyenne held her breath and listened. But he was still deeply asleep, exhaling audibly every few seconds.

She tiptoed across the floor, testing each step. Putting her hand out for the knob, she found the door was not quite closed. It was a tiny thing, but still it seemed like a good sign.

She trailed her fingers down the wall of the hall until she reached the dining room. Pinkies leading the way, she ran her hands lightly over the table and what seemed to be a sideboard, but she found nothing more than dirty dishes.

In the living room, on a rough wooden table, Cheyenne found what she was looking for. Her fingers traced the shape of it and her mind supplied the picture. A big silver wrench. Heavy. She put the piece of glass in her pocket and then picked up the wrench and thwacked the end into her palm. If she hit Griffin hard enough, she could knock him unconscious.

If she hit Griffin hard enough.

And if she didn't? Then he might wake up. Might chase her down. Might kill her.

Cheyenne could feel her heart rate speeding up, her breath quickening, all that fight-or-flight response they had learned in biology. She turned and walked back down the hall.

Outside the doorway, she stopped and listened. What if Griffin was awake and watching? What if she rushed him and he wrested the wrench from her hand and whacked her with it?

Nothing but the sound of his deep, even breathing.

She drew one last ragged breath and tiptoed toward him. Gripping the wrench in both hands, she raised it high overhead. Then, like a man splitting a log with an ax, Cheyenne swung the wrench in its swift and terrible descent.

Before They Come Back

Tears were still running down Cheyenne's face as she closed the bedroom door behind her.

Oh, God.

Oh, God.

She was pretty sure that she had just killed a man. A kid, really. Someone her own age. And the only person in this house who had treated her with kindness.

Cheyenne had meant to knock Griffin unconscious, but after she had hit him once, he had started up, yelling.

Her heart had flopped in her chest like a fish. Without thinking, she had struck him again. Much harder. He fell back on the bed. And after that, he hadn't moved. At all. She had dropped the wrench—wet now with his blood—on the floor.

Forcing her feet to move, she staggered down the hall. If she didn't hurry, the men would come back and find her.

And she knew they *would* kill her. Especially now. After what she had done.

Oh, God.

How long did she have? How long until they came back? Cheyenne tried to distract herself by figuring it out. The drop had been planned for three in the morning. And they had wanted to make sure the money wasn't being traced or monitored in any way before they picked it up. Then they would drive back here and split it up. Now it was 2:12.

Cheyenne figured she didn't have long—an hour, maybe two, no more. She had been around these men long enough to know that they would grow impatient, that their greed would trump any common sense. They wouldn't be able to watch that lonely bag of money for long before they decided they had to claim it. Before they came back here, she had to get as much distance as she could between herself and them.

She wished she had Phantom. She thought of Duke. Barking, lunging, big. Clearly bought to scare people. Cheyenne felt a flash of unexpected sympathy. You couldn't always tell what something was by looking at the outside.

In order to move with any speed, she would need something to tell her about obstacles. Her cane was a pile of melted rods inside the woodstove. What could she use as an emergency cane? While she had been lying awake, waiting for time to drag itself forward, Cheyenne had created a useless catalog of things they surely didn't have—pool cues, ski poles, walking sticks, golf umbrellas. Now she forced herself to be practical. She would have to find a long branch, break it off, and strip it of twigs.

And then Cheyenne realized what this place did have. In spades. Car antennae.

She opened the front door and walked down the three steps. Earlier, her brain had automatically counted the stairs, just as it had the number of steps from the car to the house. The air was so cold it felt like it was pulling her lungs inside out. Her breath shook every time she exhaled, but she still wouldn't let herself think about what she had just done.

Remembering that the yard had been littered with junk, she took short steps, feeling with each foot before committing her full weight. Her right arm was folded across her belly, like a bumper, and she swung her left arm like a feeler. Cheyenne was alert to every sound, every smell, every bit of information. Her orientation and mobility instructors had tried to help her learn to use blindsight—a sense some blind people had of nearby objects and even their rough dimensions. But usually she relied on a cane or a dog to give her much more accurate feedback.

After a minute or two, Cheyenne hit pay dirt. Her fingers grazed a fender. She felt along the edge of the car roof until she found the antenna. Then she snapped it off.

At the sound, barking exploded from the barn. The

chain rattled along the ground as Duke burst out and ran toward her.

Cheyenne threw her left arm over her throat and braced herself. But the impact never came. About fifteen feet from her, the barking suddenly ended abruptly with a choking sound. The dog must have reached the end of his chain. As soon as he got back on his feet, he started barking again. The noise made her wince. But there was no answering human sound. It was just the two of them, in the dark.

Cheyenne took a deep breath. Let it out. Coughed for a few seconds, then got it under control. She had to forget about everything. Ignore the dog. Not think about Griffin. Not wonder if he was dead. She had to focus on getting out of here before the men came back.

Waving the antenna in front of her, she took a few experimental steps. It wasn't nearly long enough, and it was too flexible. Still, it was a lot better than nothing. Once she reached the woods, she could replace it with a long stick.

She started off. Behind her, Duke whined, low in his throat. She realized he had stopped barking. She could hear his breathing. The sound reminded her so much of Phantom.

Cheyenne turned. Not knowing if there was a moon out or how well the dog could see in the dark, she was careful to keep her face turned to the side, so he wouldn't think she was challenging him with a stare. She kept still, with her arms at her sides.

"Good dog," she said. She stretched each word out and kept her voice soft. "Did I scare you? I didn't mean to."

Duke whined again.

Cheyenne kept her words flowing, each one slow and soothing. "Do you ever get tired of being on that big chain? Do you ever just want to get out of here? To be free?" Her voice had been trembling, but now it strengthened. It was a crazy idea, but then so was walking through the woods whacking the underbrush with a car antenna. "Do you want to just go? Do you, Duke?"

Very slowly, she reached into her coat pocket. Her fingers closed on a piece of kibble. With an underhand toss, she threw it in his direction.

A yip let her know that she had spooked him. How many times had someone shied a stone at Duke? But he must have figured out it wasn't a stone, because next he made a curious little whuff. The chain rattled, and she heard him whine as he strained forward. The kibble must be out of reach.

She threw another piece. Another whine. On the third toss, a snuffle, followed by a gobble, told her that he had managed to retrieve it.

He caught the next piece of kibble in midair. She heard the big jaws snap closed. Another low whine. Begging.

Cheyenne wondered if Duke had ever begged before in his life. Or if anyone would have listened if he had.

With each bit of kibble she took a step closer. Finally

she was close enough that she could feel his warmth. Making a fist of her hand, she held it out, still not certain that he wouldn't snap it off in a single bite. Instead he sniffed. She felt the dampness of his cold nose, and then, incredibly, a warm wet tongue. So Duke was a dog after all, despite what everyone else thought.

Moving with infinite slowness, Cheyenne placed the palm of her hand on his head. Duke trembled, but did not otherwise move or make a sound. She scratched behind one ear. When she moved her hand to his other ear, he pressed against her fingers, urging her to scratch *right there*, just as Phantom would have. She felt herself calming down, and she sensed that Duke was, too.

Tracing their way down his neck, her fingers found the place where the heavy chain clipped onto the metal choke collar with a simple toggle. Could she walk him on the chain? She took a few steps away from Duke, letting the links play through her fingers. No. The chain was far too long and heavy.

Then Cheyenne thought of her belt. She walked back to Duke and began to scratch his head again. Even though every bit of her screamed that she had to get out of here as soon as she could, she knew she couldn't hurry without risking spooking him. With her free hand, she undid her belt buckle. Awkwardly, she rolled it up one-handed, slowly slipping it loop by loop from her jeans.

She didn't want Duke to see the belt loose, in case he felt threatened. Who knew if Duke had ever been whipped?

Cheyenne amended the thought. She knew.

All the while, she kept up a steady stroking with her other hand, tracing the shape of his head. Duke, with his short, flat fur, felt nothing like Phantom, yet it was as if Phantom was with her now.

When she had the belt free, her fingers tucked the end of it underneath Duke's collar. He whined, quivering under her touch, but otherwise didn't move. Threading the belt through the metal loop, Cheyenne pulled it until it became a makeshift leash. As if she were holding Phantom, she found herself taking her normal stance, her left leg ahead of her right, with the dog's head next to her left thigh. Then she held her breath as she unclipped the chain.

"Duke, forward," she said. "Come on, let's get out of here!"

The dog whined deep in his chest but didn't move.

"Duke, forward!" she said again. "Hop up!" Phantom would have known that meant she wanted to go fast, but what did Duke know? Then she felt him gather himself.

And they were off.

The Wind Creates the Trees

One thing Cheyenne hadn't thought about when she made her impulsive decision was that Duke wouldn't "clear" her. Phantom had been taught to watch out for low-hanging branches or other objects that might hit Cheyenne even if they missed him. Duke had no idea. And neither did Cheyenne, at least not until she ended up with a deep scratch on one cheek. After that, she put her right hand up about a foot in front of her face, trying to gain a second's warning.

Cheyenne had pointed Duke toward the woods, not knowing if he would follow her suggestion, but he had. She had felt him curve around the house and then head into the trees. The ground was crisp with frost, but with a springy softness underneath from decades of pine needles.

Even knowing that daylight would bring far greater danger, Cheyenne found herself missing the little sight she had. Which way was Duke taking her? She could only follow the sway of the dog and listen to what her body told her. Her joints let her know whether she was going uphill or down, turning right or left. When you were sighted, you didn't pay attention to such messages because you didn't need to. When you were blind, you discovered your body had been saying these things all along.

Now Cheyenne felt a branch brush the top of her head. But at least it hadn't gone through her head. Duke had led her around a tree, Cheyenne realized. "Good dog," she said.

Duke made a noise, low in his throat. It sounded like a question.

"Yes, you are a good dog." She didn't know if that was the question, or if he was asking if he could trust her, or whether Duke wanted to know if they should keep moving.

Cheyenne just knew that the answer was yes.

They walked for a long time. It was slow going. Her shoes kept slipping off, until finally she took the remnant of cord still tied around one ankle, cut it in two, and then threaded the pieces through the top holes of her shoes, tying each in a double knot. They went on, pushing their way through undergrowth, her feet catching on roots and downed branches. Sometimes she had to stop because she would start to cough and then not be able to catch her breath. The cold air seared her lungs. Hoping it would warm the air, she wrapped her scarf over her mouth and nose, leaving just her eyes uncovered.

The wind was so cold it felt like it cut right through her, but it also helped her picture the outside world. She could hear the rustling of the trees now. In a way, the wind created the trees. Without the wind it was like there were no trees at all, at least not until their branches scraped her face or arms.

Occasionally Cheyenne felt the face of her watch. By the time it got light, she hoped she might find the road that Griffin had told her about.

Surely the men had returned by now. And they had found Griffin. She tried not to think about what she had done to him. And now they would hunt her down. As long as it was dark, she might have a slight advantage. The problem was that there was no way she and Duke were covering even two miles an hour. Probably much less.

It got a little easier as they went deeper and deeper into the woods. There seemed to be fewer bushes. The bottoms of her pants flapped stiffly, soaked from pushing through undergrowth. So were her shoes.

They kept plodding forward. Her legs were so tired they felt bruised, and her feet were frozen stumps. She tried to wiggle her toes and couldn't.

Was it starting to get light? All she could see out of her left eye was a hazy grayness. Cheyenne checked her watch. It was a little after 7 A.M. Probably not yet. But soon.

Duke whined.

Cheyenne froze. "What is it, boy?" she whispered. She heard a rustle in the bushes to their left. *Oh, crap. This was it.* They had found her.

Duke barked. Instinctively, she tried to put her hand

over his snout, but he nipped at it. She jerked her hand back, surprised. For a moment, she had forgotten it was Duke she was with, not Phantom.

Then several things happened at once.

Straining forward, Duke unleashed a volley of barks.

Something exploded from the bushes and ran right in front of them. Part of Cheyenne relaxed as she heard the underbrush rattle. Whatever it was, it was small. Definitely not a person. Probably a rabbit or squirrel or maybe even a chipmunk.

Still barking, Duke lunged after it.

The belt jerked in her hand. And then it was gone.

And so was Duke.

"Come back!" Cheyenne shouted, suddenly frantic. "Duke! Duke!"

She could tell from the pitch of his barking that he was running away from her. Fast. He was already at least a hundred feet away. Cheyenne opened her mouth to try calling him again. Then she realized that all she was accomplishing was to advertise her presence. Probably for miles.

Taking a deep, shuddering breath, Cheyenne told herself that she was on her own now. That was a fact and she couldn't change it, only deal with it. She touched her watch face. It was 7:33. She was pretty sure that they had been traveling roughly northwest. The grayness she could see with her left eye was just getting lighter. Using the trunk of a tree to orient herself, she slowly turned in a circle until she confirmed that east—where there was more light—was where she thought it was. Crouching, Cheyenne groped until she found several long branches. She picked the longest and sturdiest, and then snapped off the smaller twigs. It was hard work. Her right hand was stiff with cold, and her left hand, the one that had been holding the makeshift leash, refused to move much at all. She brought it up to her cheek. It felt as if a branch was brushing her face. Her cheek could feel her icy fingers, but not the other way around. The bottoms of her pants now had a crackly coating of ice.

After several long minutes, the branch was free of twigs. It wasn't a dog, and it was barely a cane, but it would have to do. When Cheyenne finally straightened up, her knees had locked. She staggered forward a few steps.

She couldn't feel her feet or the tops of her ears. Her left hand was in her pocket, but it still felt dead and stiff. And now her right hand was slowly freezing, making it hard to hold the makeshift cane. Cheyenne continued to tap her way forward, turning her head from side to side, alert for the sounds that reflected back to her, trying to sense objects before she ran into them. Sometimes she just missed a tree or bush at the last moment. Sometimes she tripped over stones or roots.

Without the company of Duke, Cheyenne was aware of how alone she was. Every sound made her freeze. Could there be large animals in these woods—coyotes or even mountain lions? But the animals that really scared her were the two-legged ones. A crow exploded out of the bushes ahead of her, and she cried out at the sound of its harsh call, the flap of its wings.

Every creak or rustle behind her was one of her kidnappers. Each time she heard a noise, Cheyenne took a deep breath and forced herself to keep moving forward, trying to make her steps as light as possible. She walked with her head turned to one side, straining to use her left eye as she never had before. Now that it was lighter, she could see just enough to keep from blundering into tree trunks, but not enough to avoid low-hanging branches.

Her chest ached, and every few minutes she found herself coughing. Each time it was harder to stop. She wanted to lie down. If you froze to death, didn't you just go to sleep and never wake up? That way, it wouldn't even hurt. The idea seemed appealing.

A tiny cold dot landed on her cheek, then another in her eyelashes. Snow. It fell faster, softly freckling her face. At home, she hated snow. All her familiar markings, the different textures of grass and gravel, asphalt and concrete, were obliterated. If the snow was deep enough to cover the curb, she had to stay home, because she couldn't tell one block from another.

Here in the forest, the snow presented a different problem. Soon, with every step, Cheyenne would leave a footprint.

And then it would be a simple matter for them to track her down.

Coming Closer by the Second

Cheyenne had been walking by herself for about half an hour when she heard something moving in the woods behind her. Not making any effort to be quiet. And this time there was no doubt as to what it was.

A human. And coming closer by the second.

Panicked, Cheyenne began a blundering search for shelter. She found a clutch of something that still had leaves, some kind of low bush. Pushing aside branches, she scrambled in. She paid no attention to how it scratched her face and neck, or the wetness that soaked through to her knees. And still, when she was in as deep as she could get, she wondered if her silver coat was shining through a thin patch, or if her shoe was sticking out.

The footsteps came closer and stopped. She could hear someone's harsh breathing. A man's. She knew it wasn't a lost hunter. And it certainly wasn't someone come to rescue her or they would have been calling out for her. That left only three choices. But which of the three men was it? Roy, TJ, or Jimbo? And did it really matter? Or would she be dead no matter who it was? She remembered TJ's rank breath when he straddled her. Maybe the real horror would be how long she was alive before she was dead.

It was so hard to hold absolutely still while every molecule of her being screamed that she should run away. How much snow was on the ground? Did her footprints lead straight to her, like an arrow? She was barely breathing.

And then Cheyenne felt it. A cough. Forcing its way out of her throat. Her eyes watered. She bit her lip. She couldn't cough. She couldn't. A cough would be her death sentence. The coppery taste of blood washed across her tongue as she bit down harder and harder.

Then the cough pushed its way up out of her chest, tore through her throat, and shattered the silence.

And the footsteps charged toward her.

"No!" Cheyenne screamed. "No! No!" Strong arms lifted her off her feet, and a calloused hand went across her mouth. She struggled, kicking and flailing, but all she did was tire herself out. And she was already so tired.

"Cheyenne!" a voice said. "Sh, sh. Calm down."

Griffin?

She started to cough again. He dropped his arms and stepped back, leaving her standing.

Cheyenne coughed so hard that she staggered sideways.

Finally she managed to gasp, "You're alive!" In a weird way, it was a relief to know she hadn't killed him.

"No thanks to you." His voice was matter-of-fact.

The reality of her situation set in. "Oh," Cheyenne said. "Right. They sent you out after me, didn't they?" She realized there was no use running anymore, no use fighting. She had done her best. She had done more than she had ever thought possible. But it hadn't been enough. "Go ahead," she said. "Do what you have to do." She took a deep breath and braced herself.

"What are you talking about?" Griffin asked. "Go ahead with what?"

Cheyenne didn't understand why he was stretching this out. He must want revenge for her attack. "You're going to shoot me, right? Just get it over with."

"Why do you think I'm going to shoot you?"

"Oh, don't pretend. TJ told me I was going to die. You guys have to kill me so I can't lead the cops back to you." She swallowed. In a few more seconds, she would break down and start to beg. And that's how she would die, begging and choking on her own blood. No. She wouldn't. She tried to make her voice light, as if this wasn't really happening. Maybe she could pretend right up until the very end. "So go ahead. Do what you need to do. Just make it fast." She took a deep breath and then closed her eyes so that she was in complete blackness. She tried to picture her mother's face. I'm coming, Mom.

There was a long silence. When it was broken, it was not by a gunshot, but by Griffin's voice, weary and disappointed.

"I'm out here trying to help you, not kill you. I came after you on my own. But I don't think TJ and Jimbo and my dad can be that far behind. So we've got to get out of here as fast as we can. Get to the road, flag someone down for help, and go to the cops."

"Wait. You came out here to help me? After what I did to you?"

"When I first woke up I was pretty pissed off. I've got a bloody bump on top of my head the size of an egg, and it throbs every time my heart beats." Griffin's voice was tinged with bitterness. "I was actually planning on helping you get away. If you had given me a few more minutes, my alarm would have gone off. I didn't tell you because I didn't know if I could trust you not to let it slip. Besides, part of me couldn't believe they would really do anything that drastic. Not really. But then after you hit me with that wrench, I realized that everyone is capable of violence. Even you. Even my dad. And that I was naïve to think that they would really let you go. So my choices were to sit at home and wait, or to find you and help you escape. You know, wandering alone out in the woods in the middle of a snowstorm when you're blind and have pneumonia is not a really good escape plan." He let out a long, exasperated sigh. "How could you really believe that I'm some stone-cold killer?"

"What about that gun you held to my head in the car? Remember?"

"Oh. That." His voice sounded oddly embarrassed. "That wasn't a real gun."

Not a real gun? "Well, then, what was it?"

"That was actually the cigarette lighter from the dash."

Cheyenne remembered the circle of cold metal pressed against her temple. "A cigarette lighter?" She had been so scared.

"Sorry." He took her arm. "Come on. We'd better start moving before they catch up with us. You can tell the cops that I helped you. And that I never meant for this to happen."

Cheyenne didn't move. "Won't you get in a lot of trouble?"

"I think it's a little bit late for me to be thinking about that. I'm already in trouble. It's just a matter of how bad. So let's get going."

Face the Facts

Two hours earlier, Griffin had woken up with one hell of a headache. The alarm was buzzing, and he had a blurry feeling that it had been going off for a while.

Before he had lain down beside Cheyenne, he had set the alarm for two thirty. He was sure it wouldn't be necessary, that he would be too keyed up to sleep.

And that was his last waking thought.

Now the clock said it was 3:12 A.M. He sat up. A wave of dizziness crashed over him. His head ached something fierce. When he put his hand to the top of his head, it came away wet and sticky.

At the sight of the red on his fingers, he felt a muzzy sort of shock. He explored the wound more gingerly. Two welts, one an inch longer, right next to each other. The skin around them was swollen tight. But no broken bits of bone when he probed, grinding his teeth together against the pain. Pushing himself into a sitting position, Griffin tried to figure out what had happened. He was on the bed, in his sleeping bag. He looked to his left. The nylon cord was still tied to the empty bed, but there was no Cheyenne on the end of it. And on the floor was a big silver wrench, one end clotted with something. He felt a little sick when he looked at the reddish brown clump, matted with hair. That was blood. *His* blood.

Griffin got up. For a second, he had to steady himself on the bedpost. He wasn't going to make the same mistake he had last time. He wasn't going to go rushing outside only to leave Cheyenne in the house. He quickly went from room to room, opening all the closets and looking underneath the furniture. The fire in the woodstove had gone out, and the house was quiet and cold.

No Cheyenne. This time she really had to be in the woods. He yanked on a coat, hat, and gloves, then grabbed the flashlight and went looking for her. And then he discovered Duke was gone, too. To follow their trail, he had been forced to move slowly, scanning back and forth with his flashlight, looking for a footprint in the dusting of snow, or freshly broken branches. Once it got light, Griffin knew it would be easier—for everyone. He had been determined to find her before the others did.

Now he walked beside Cheyenne through the forest. Even though it was daylight, it was the time of year when even at noon the light was gray and uncertain. Scarves of mist clung to the trees. Sounds carried oddly here, floating through the cold, crisp air, making it hard to pinpoint where they came from. Even though he was hurrying as fast as he could, it was still slow going as they skirted mud holes and underbrush.

At least the snow was lighter here, just a spotty dusting, so they didn't have to worry about leaving tracks. There wasn't enough clear space for them to easily walk side by side, so while Griffin carefully steered Cheyenne across relatively unlittered ground, his own feet scuffed through ferns or got sucked in by half-frozen mud.

When his foot was wrenched from under him, Griffin screamed. He couldn't help it. He fell to the ground.

"What is it?" Cheyenne yelled. Her hands swam through the air, looking for him. "Griffin? What's wrong?"

The pain was so great that he couldn't speak. Hot tears ran down his cheeks. He pushed himself up on his elbows. His left foot was still half in the hole he had stepped in, some animal's small burrow. But his leg was now facing a completely different direction.

"Griffin?" Cheyenne's voice broke. Her unseeing eyes were wide as she turned her head from side to side.

"It's my ankle," he managed to grunt. "I stepped in a hole, and I think I broke it."

Invisible knives were slicing his tendons and nerves.

Griffin didn't mean to, but when he pulled his foot free of the hole, he let out another scream. It dangled at the end of his leg like a shoe he had half kicked off. But this was his foot. Panting, Griffin pulled up his pants leg, ignoring the fresh waves of agony, even though part of him didn't want to know how damaged it was.

Cheyenne found his shoulder and crouched beside him. "How bad is it?"

"Bad. My foot's pointing the wrong way."

"Is it bleeding?"

"No. But I think at least one of the bones in my ankle is broken."

"What are we going to do?" Cheyenne's face was creased with concern.

It was hard to think. Griffin realized he was moaning faintly at the end of every breath. "Here. Help me get up. If I can lean on you, maybe I can hop on my good leg. I'm going to have to be your eyes, and you're going to have to help be my leg."

Cheyenne leaned down. Putting her hands around his wrists, she began to pull while Griffin tried to stand on just his right leg. She was overbalanced, in danger of toppling onto him. He got nearly all the way up and then lurched forward. His left foot touched the ground. A bolt of electricity jolted its way up his leg, burning every nerve. With a cry, he fell back on the ground, pulling Cheyenne over on top of him. He let out another scream when some part of her pressed against his ankle. He was in too much pain to be ashamed. She rolled off him so they were lying next to each other on the icy ground. For a second, there was just the sound of their breathing.

He made himself face the facts. "I can't do it, Cheyenne. You'll have to go on on your own."

She propped herself on one elbow. "I'm not leaving you here. You could freeze to death. I can already hear your teeth chattering."

"It's nothing. Just from the shock, that's all." He was vaguely aware of the cold and wet seeping through his pants. "Look, we're only about a mile or two from the main road. I can point you in the right direction. Just keep walking in a straight line, and you should get there in less than an hour. That's not enough time for anything bad to happen to me. Face it. There's no way I can put any weight on my leg. Even if I managed to get to my feet, I can't hop for two miles. You go out to the road and flag somebody down. Then you can come back for me."

She trailed her fingers up his chest until she found his face, then cupped his cheek. "But if they find you, they might kill you for helping me."

"But they won't know that I was helping you." He had to speak through gritted teeth as the pain seared up his leg and into his brain. "I'll just tell them I was looking for you. And then I'll say I saw tracks going in the completely opposite direction."

"No." She shook her head, her upper lip curled. "No way." She grabbed one of his hands and half stood. "I can't leave you here. You have to come with me. Come on. Just try getting up again. You gave up too soon." Her face was so white. A blue vein fluttered in her temple.

"Cheyenne"—he hardened his voice—"I can't. If either one of us is going to survive, you have to get to that road as soon as possible."

A Quarter-Million Dollars, Two Guns, and a Dead Man

Griffin was so cold. His whole body vibrated. And each time he shivered, it ran down his leg to his ankle. It felt like the ends of the bone were grating together, but he couldn't stop shaking. He remembered shaking like this in the burn unit. The nurses had told him it was shock and then wrapped the unburned parts of his body in white blankets warm from a special dryer.

He tried to tense his body so that he would stop shaking, but it didn't help. Every shiver was echoed by a wave of pain that radiated from his ankle to his pelvis. Trying to conserve the little heat he had, Griffin curled on his side. But he was still just as cold, if not worse, and now a new side of him was wet. The backs of his clothes were already stiffening with ice.

He didn't know how long he lay there before something roused him out of himself. At first Griffin thought he was imagining it, but then he definitely heard something. He corrected the thought. Someone. Moving through the forest. And voices, too. He couldn't make out any words, but the tones were familiar—Jimbo and TJ. Arguing. That was familiar too.

"We just go back to the house and take the truck and go," said Jimbo. "Go before Roy has a chance to rethink this. Screw them. We've got our money."

"But where are we supposed to go?" TJ sounded confused.

"Don't you get it? There isn't any more 'supposed to.' We can do what we want. We each have a quarter of a million dollars. I think I'm going to Brazil. I've always wanted to go to Carnaval."

"What about TJ?"

"What about you?" Jimbo echoed.

"Am I going with you?"

Jimbo didn't say anything for a few seconds. Then he said, "Maybe it's time we did things on our own."

"Hey!" Griffin yelled. "Hey!" He levered himself up on one elbow, ignoring how much it hurt to move.

"What the hell was that?" TJ sounded spooked.

"It's Griffin, dummy," Jimbo said. "Hey, Griff—where are you?"

"Over here. I'm hurt."

A few seconds later, they were standing over him.

"Well, well, well. What happened here?" Jimbo seemed to be dressed in every coat he owned. He stood with one fist on his hip. The other hand held a rifle. TJ stood two paces behind, holding his own gun.

"I'm hurt. I was trying to track Cheyenne down when I stepped into a hole." Griffin pointed. "My ankle's broken." He looked past them. "Where's my dad?"

"Driving the roads, looking for her," TJ said. Turning to Jimbo, he took a cell phone from his pocket. "Should we call Roy?"

"You're going to have to call someone," Griffin said. "I can't walk. You need to get someone out here to help me."

"Hold on a minute, Teej." Jimbo cocked his head. "Where's Cheyenne?"

"She hit me in the head and knocked me out. Didn't you see my note?"

"We saw the note." TJ leaned closer to look at Griffin's ankle. He shook his head. "Did you find her?"

"I was getting close right before I stepped into the hole. I could hear her over there." Griffin pointed in the opposite direction from the way Cheyenne had gone. "But before you go looking for her, could you call my dad?"

"He's busy, like we are," Jimbo said. "Trying to find the stupid girl you let slip through your fingers."

Griffin didn't like the way this was going. "Then could you carry me out? I can't put any weight on my foot at all."

TJ stretched his free hand in Griffin's direction, but Jimbo touched his arm, and he stopped. Then Jimbo pointed at something with the nose of his rifle.

"What's that?"

Griffin looked. Lying next to him was the striped scarf Cheyenne had worn around her neck. It must have come off when she lost her balance and fell, trying to help him up.

"I—I don't know."

"Hey, that's Cheyenne's," TJ said slowly. "I thought you said you didn't catch up to her."

"I didn't." It seemed painfully clear he was lying. "She just dropped it here, and I found it." It made sense, but he should have said it first thing. Now they would figure out he had let her go.

"You just found it," Jimbo said. "Lying in the bushes?"

"Yeah. That's how I knew I was getting close."

"Okay, Griff, what really happened? Did you get her back for whacking you upside the head?" Jimbo grinned. "I guess the apple doesn't fall far from the tree." He looked around. "So where did you put her?"

"What are you talking about?"

TJ shook his head. "Never mind," he said. "It's nothing you need to know."

Jimbo looked back at Griffin, a sly grin playing across his face. "Where do you think your mama's been all these years?"

"Chicago," Griffin said, but when he said the word out loud, it seemed silly somehow. "With her family." He had always wondered if she had remarried, maybe had another family. A kid who didn't have scars.

"I told you, don't tell him," TJ said urgently. "He doesn't need to know."

Jimbo didn't pay any attention. "Chicago?" he echoed Griffin sarcastically. "Uh-huh. Eating deep-dish pizza and listening to jazz?"

"Why?" Griffin sat all the way up, ignoring the screaming pain in his leg. "Is she, like, in Portland or something?"

"Portland. That's a good one," Jimbo muttered. "Portland."

TJ sighed. "She's been out in the back, Griffin, underneath a Honda quarter panel. We buried her out there."

"What?" Griffin didn't even feel shock. He just felt—nothing. Like he was falling, and there would never be anything to catch him.

"Roy's always had a temper, you know that," Jimbo said, shrugging. "Well, things went crossways between him and Janie when you were in the hospital. She was always ragging on him about you getting burned. And one night he gave her a little shove when she had been getting into his face. She tripped and her head hit the fireplace. He left her there to teach her a lesson, and went to bed. And when he got up, she was stone-cold dead."

"No," Griffin said. He shook his head violently, not caring that it might jostle his leg. "No." Even though he could picture it in his head, even though he could see it more clearly than he could see Jimbo and TJ. He started to stand, needing to get to his feet, and then fell back with a cry. His mother was dead?

"Look at him," Jimbo said in a flat, unaccented voice, like a hypnotist's. "If we leave him here, then how long is

he going to last? I mean, look at him." TJ turned and together the two men regarded Griffin as calmly as if he were
something they had found by the side of the road. "His
skin's already kind of blue. We'll just tell Roy we never saw
him and let nature take its course. And that way we'll know
he'll never tell anybody about the money."

It was like Griffin wasn't even there.

TJ cocked his head to one side. "But what about Roy?"

"That's not our problem, dummy," Jimbo said. "If he
wants to come out in the woods and start looking, then so
be it. We'll be long gone by then."

"You're just going to let him freeze to death?" TJ seemed
to have finally grasped what Jimbo was saying.

"He's already halfway there," Jimbo said calmly. "Why
do we have to intervene?"

Griffin thought it couldn't get much worse, but his
blood turned to ice at TJ's next words.

"Jeez, if I had a dog like that, I'd shoot him." TJ pointed
his handgun at Griffin's midsection.

Griffin froze.

Jimbo pushed the barrel of the gun aside. "Don't be
stupid. You do that, they'll go looking for who shot him.
You leave him just like he is, and it will be clear what happened. He caught his foot in a hole, he broke his ankle, and
he died. End of story. Nobody asks any questions, and nobody's in trouble."

"I'm not stupid. We'll bury him out here. I'm tired of
you saying I'm stupid."

Griffin's hand closed on a fist-sized rock. It was ridiculous—like using a slingshot against a bazooka—but he wasn't going to die just lying on his back on the icy ground.

"I told you," TJ repeated when Jimbo didn't respond. "Don't call me stupid."

"Why not? It's the truth." Jimbo shrugged. "You *are* stupid. It's way too much work to bury him. But that's just like you—you never think things through."

Then a gun went off. And Griffin's heart stopped.

But it was Jimbo who collapsed on the pine needles.

"There," TJ said. "Who's stupid now? Who's stupid now, Jimbo?" He was breathing hard.

Griffin's ears were ringing. He did not move a muscle. He was dead now. It was only a matter of time until TJ made it official.

But then TJ dropped the gun and leaned over, his hands on his knees. Vomit splattered on the pine needles.

Griffin cut his eyes toward Jimbo and then wished he hadn't. He adjusted his head a couple of inches so that he wouldn't accidentally see the body again.

Straightening up, TJ wiped the back of his mouth with his hand. "I've never done that before," he said. "It's different than you think."

Griffin was afraid to even meet TJ's eyes. When he finally did, he saw TJ's pupils looked too big. And his face looked like he was about ready to laugh or cry—or both.

"Oh, well," TJ said, "there is one good thing. Jimbo

finally, finally shut up." His laugh was high-pitched. It sounded like glass breaking.

Griffin heard TJ go over to the body, but he still refused to look. Jimbo had landed on his side. He heard TJ pull the backpack off Jimbo's back.

TJ walked back into Griffin's line of sight. "It's half yours," he said, hefting the backpack.

"That's okay. I don't need any."

TJ unzipped the backpack. There was a long silence. "It's wet. Why is the money all wet?" His voice arced higher. He reached in and grabbed a fistful of money, pulled it out. Red drops speckled the snow. "It's blood. Oh, my God, it's blood!"

He dropped the money and then the backpack. A bill floated down and landed by Griffin's hand. One end of it looked like it had been dipped in red paint.

TJ found a little patch of snow. He knelt down and began to wipe his hands on it like it was a towel. Washing his hands in snow. It quickly turned slushy and pink. And then he stood up, without saying another word to Griffin, and walked away. Leaving Griffin with a broken ankle, a bloody backpack filled with a quarter of a million dollars, two guns, and a dead man.

The Hardest Thing in the World

Crouched behind a huge tree, Cheyenne tried to be as quiet as possible. She was too winded to hold her breath, so she panted shallowly, openmouthed. The cold air scraped her lungs. Her eyes watered, but she refused to cough. Any second they would find her. Thirty minutes ago she had heard the sound of a gunshot, not close, but not far away, either. It had spurred her to walk even faster.

Then five minutes ago she had heard the faint sound of a car engine. She must be near the road! That meant there were people up ahead, people who could help her. And then this whole long ordeal would be over.

She had hurried forward, mindless of branches that lashed her legs, of ground so rough she stumbled and nearly fell a half-dozen times. Her only thought had been to flag down the driver, even though part of her knew that he was surely long gone.

But then she had heard it. Someone running through the trees. Running right for her. And who else would be out in the woods? The driver of the car wouldn't suddenly get out, because he wouldn't have any idea she was here. It must be one of the three men. She had gotten lucky when Griffin had turned out to be one of the good guys.

She didn't think she would get lucky twice.

So Cheyenne had hidden behind the biggest tree she could find and concentrated on remaining absolutely still.

It was the hardest thing in the world. She wanted to jump up and start waving her arms and screaming. Just to get the inevitable over with. Was her killer even now aiming a gun at her?

Cheyenne tried to think of a plan. Knowing she was probably going to die gave her a certain amount of freedom. Maybe she could rush whoever it was—TJ, Jimbo, or Roy— and wrestle the gun away before he overcame his amazement at her suicidal charge. Although it was more likely that she would just end up with a fist-sized hole in her chest.

Still, something inside of her refused to give up. Not after she had gotten so far, risked so much, done so many things she would have said were impossible just a week earlier.

Then words rang out through the cold, still air.

"Freeze! Police! Hold it right there!"

An electric shock jolted from Cheyenne's head to her heels.

Not the bad guys, then.

Cheyenne was going to live. She had made it!

She didn't obey the cop. She couldn't. She stood up and ran toward his voice, heedless of what might be in her way.

"Help me, oh, please help me!" Something sharp tore through her pants, gouging her left calf. Shaking herself free, she ran on, holding her hands high overhead so he would know she didn't constitute a threat. Her only goal was to close the gap between herself and the cop as fast as she could. She wanted to finally be safe. "Help me!" she yelled again. "I've been kidnapped."

A firm hand gripped her shoulder. "Slow down there, little lady. What are you saying?" There was a faint sound of amusement in the cop's rough voice. Did he think she was playing some kind of game?

"I'm Cheyenne Wilder. I was kidnapped from the Woodlands Experience shopping mall two days ago."

"Wait a minute—they mentioned you at roll call this morning. Are you really Cheyenne Wilder? The daughter of Nike's president?" She could feel him inspecting her. Cheyenne imagined how she must look, her clothes muddy and torn, her face scratched, and her tangled curls filled with old leaves, pine needles, and broken sticks. But her appearance would serve as proof. The only way anyone could look the way she did was if she had been running blind through the woods all night long.

"Jeez," he said, half to himself. His voice was hoarse,

like he was just getting over a cold. "I'm out looking for people jacking deer and instead I find the girl they're searching for in three states." She heard his feet shift, and she imagined him looking around. "Where are these guys? Did they follow you?"

"No, no. I was so afraid." A little sigh escaped her now that she could let go of the fear. "I was so afraid you were one of them. I thought they had finally found me."

He let out a two-note laugh. "Don't worry. I've got you now. You're safe. I'd better call in with the good news." She heard him punch some buttons. "Guess who I've got? Cheyenne Wilder! And she appears to be in good condition. Over."

She could hear a faint, tinny voice, but couldn't make out the words.

"Roger that," the cop said. "You can stop searching for her."

"Let me talk to my father," she begged, holding out her empty hand. "Please."

"Oh, he's not at my station, Cheyenne." Then the cop spoke to the voice at the other end of the line. "Could you get in contact with Mr. Wilder and have him ring me back? Someone here would very much like to speak to him. Meanwhile, I'm bringing her in. Over and out." His voice changed, and she could tell he was talking to her again. "My car's about a half mile down the road. Do you think you could walk there if I guided you?"

"I just made it through the woods. A road's no problem." There was no way Cheyenne was going to let the cop get more than five feet from her. She couldn't stand the idea of being alone, even for a second. What if one of the men popped out of the woods behind her while she was waiting?

He took her elbow, and they began to walk. They hadn't gone more than a hundred paces when their feet crunched on gravel and then, a few steps later, on smooth blacktop. They had reached the road. So Cheyenne hadn't been imagining it when she thought she heard a car. If the cop hadn't come along, she still might have been able to flag down someone. At least now she didn't have to worry about getting accidentally run over in the process.

"You said you escaped the men who kidnapped you. How did you do that? Did you have help?"

Cheyenne stopped in her tracks, causing the man to bump into her. "Oh, my God! I should have told you right away. You need to call out a search party. This guy Griffin is out in the woods someplace. He's hurt. He told me to go on without him and he would draw them away." Turning, she put her free hand on the cop's wrist. "He needs medical attention immediately." She tried not to think of him dead, but immediately she saw Griffin in her mind's eye, as clearly as she had seen him when they had been talking in his bedroom. He lay flat on his back on the frozen ground, his skin as pale as wax, his wide eyes staring up at the gray sky.

He's alive, Cheyenne scolded herself. *He's alive, and you'd better start laying the groundwork with the police now. If not for acquittal, then maybe probation.*

"Griffin's just this kid who lives at the house where I was being held. His father was the one who demanded the ransom money. And there were two other men there. Griffin protected me from them." Cheyenne felt her cheeks get hot. Would he think she had been raped? "He kept me safe. But the men decided they weren't going to let me go, in case I could identify them. Griffin found out what they were planning, so he helped me get away." Cheyenne decided not to mention who had kidnapped her, hoping it might help Griffin. "Please, please, you have to ask them to go out and find him."

"Are his injuries life threatening?" There was a strange note in the cop's voice.

"No. But his ankle is broken, so he can't walk. You need to find him soon, before he freezes to death."

"We'll handle that once we get back to the station." The cop didn't sound too forgiving. Cheyenne hoped whoever really decided these things would look more favorably on Griffin. "All right. Here's the car." His steps slowed, and he led her back onto the gravel.

"I've never ridden in a cop car before."

"I'm afraid you're still going to miss your chance—we use private vehicles when we work undercover." He opened the door and guided her in, his hand on the small of her back.

She sat on the front bench seat. Inside, it smelled like cigarettes and fast food. Her feet scuffled wrappers and hard things that clunked—some kind of tools?—before finding a place to rest. She heard the cop get in the other side and close the door, felt his weight settle in beside her.

"So are you taking me home?"

"Back to the station. Your dad will meet us there. We need to, um, debrief you." There was something slightly off about his voice.

Everything was slightly off, Cheyenne realized. She sniffed. Inside the confines of the car, she could smell something familiar about the cop. She sniffed again. It was the sharp, medicinal smell of peppermint overlaying the earthy smell of tobacco.

Nothing Like a Toy

Oh, no.

Cheyenne flashed back to a hard voice demanding all her phone numbers. Griffin's dad had smelled like that.

Roy hadn't needed to change his appearance. He just changed his voice, pitching it lower. But what he couldn't change was his smell.

Cheyenne knew Roy was going to drive her to her death.

Shoot her here and he might attract attention. Plus, he would be left with a bloody mess in his car. He must be planning to drive her to the house, all the while chattering about what they would do "back at the station."

She remembered the cell phone he had been using. Maybe she could snatch it and call 9-1-1. Maybe if she was really lucky, he wouldn't notice that she had it and she could hold it behind her back while she pressed the numbers. She might even buy a second or two before he heard the voice of the operator or noticed what she was doing.

It was hopeless, but what else could she do? If she got out and ran, he would tackle her in a moment and drag her back. Give up on all pretense.

The engine started up. Cheyenne swept her left hand over the seat between them. Her fingers closed over what they found.

Only it wasn't a phone.

It was a gun.

"Hey!" Roy sounded surprised. Too surprised to keep using his phony voice.

Cheyenne transferred the gun to her right hand. It wasn't very big. But it felt heavy and real and nothing like a toy. Did it have a safety?

"You make one move, and I'll shoot you."

She had wanted to make her voice full of authority, unwavering. Instead it came out high-pitched and shaking.

Roy's only answer was a laugh.

Something streaked across the small slice of vision Cheyenne still had left. Roy's hand, trying to grab the gun from her. Her finger tightened on the trigger just as his hand closed around her fist.

The sound of the gun firing was so loud that it sucked all other sounds after it.

And then the silence was broken by Roy's scream.

"You *shot* me!" He sounded more affronted than injured.

How badly was he hurt? Bad enough that he would die? Or not bad enough to keep him from hurting her?

Cheyenne realized she was still holding the gun.

"Get out!" she screamed.

"What?"

"Get out of the car! Or I'll shoot you again." She pressed the gun forward until it touched flesh. Wet flesh.

"Okay, okay!"

She heard the door open and Roy scramble out. An "oof" as he fell onto the road. Still holding the gun, Cheyenne leaned forward, found the door handle, and yanked it closed. A second later she snapped down the lock, just before Roy grabbed the handle from the outside. Now that the gun barrel was no longer dimpling his flesh, he was obviously rethinking having left the car. And he wanted back in.

The other door! Cheyenne leaned to her right, found the lock just in time. Her hand was sticky. It must be blood. The passenger door rattled.

"Let me in, Cheyenne."

"No!"

"Come on, I'm hurt. I need to get to a doctor. Let me in and I'll drive us to a hospital and let you go."

Where had she shot him? Cheyenne didn't know. His arm? His belly? His chest? It seemed quite possible that Roy was telling the truth. Maybe he did need to get to a hospital.

"Cheyenne—I'm going to bleed to death. Please, for the love of God . . ."

Slowly, she raised her hand.

He must have come back to the other side of the car,

because suddenly the driver's side door began to jiggle, making her jump.

"Let me in, Cheyenne!" His voice was louder and angrier now. "Let me in or you'll be sorry!"

Or maybe she had just nicked him.

A sudden loud bang, right next to her ear, made her scream.

It happened again. Roy was, Cheyenne realized, hammering the window with a rock. A big rock.

The third time he did it, the thump sounded more muffled. It was followed by a curse and the sound of the rock falling to the ground. He had smashed his own fingers instead of the window.

Good.

Cheyenne pressed the tip of the gun up against the glass near where she thought Roy was. She pressed hard to try to keep her hand from shaking. "Stop doing that or I'll shoot you again!"

"Really?" Roy laughed. "I don't think so. You'll miss me by a mile. Or maybe the bullet will ricochet and hit you. So go ahead." And then he smashed the rock down again.

Driving Blind

As she pressed the nose of the gun against the window, Cheyenne realized Roy was right. Even if the bullet didn't ricochet—and she wasn't quite sure how that worked— even if it did go through the window, wouldn't she still be cut by flying glass? And Roy probably wouldn't even be hurt. All she would accomplish would be to create a huge gaping hole. And then he could get her.

Frustrated and afraid, Cheyenne started to cry.

The rock banged against the window again, making her jump. Her foot touched the accelerator, and the car engine raced.

She had to do something, but what?

Then she had a sudden memory. Her mom sitting beside her, letting Cheyenne drive around the empty winding roads of a nearby cemetery on a damp Saturday afternoon.

Could she just drive away?

Another bang. It was only a matter of time before the window cracked and then broke.

Okay. She could do this. The engine was still on. Cheyenne turned in the seat and set down the gun. Her hands gripped the steering wheel so tightly that it cut into her fingers.

She quickly rehearsed what she remembered. The accelerator was on the right. The brake on the left.

But wait. The car was clearly in park now. And Cheyenne needed it to be in drive. But the one car she had driven had been an automatic. What if this was a stick? She had no idea how to use a clutch.

Leaning forward, Cheyenne felt to her right. No gearshift knob. Just the hump in the middle of the floor. The car must be an automatic. But where was the lever to change gears?

The rock banged down again.

Another flash of memory. Her grandma's old car, so old it didn't have seat belts. And the shifter was on top of the steering wheel. Sending up a silent prayer, Cheyenne pushed down one of the wands branching off the steering column. In answer, a sweeping sound. The windshield wipers.

"Hey!" Roy yelled. "Hey!"

She pushed the lever back up. The second wand felt thicker. It shifted down a notch with a satisfying clunk. Then the car moved, all right, but it bumped backward.

Cheyenne jammed both feet on the brake.

"Hey!" Roy yelled again. "What the hell do you think you're doing?"

What *was* she doing? This was ridiculous. Maybe she should just give up.

She saw movement in her sliver of vision, so it wasn't a surprise when the rock slammed down on the window again. Only this time, Cheyenne thought she heard a cracking sound.

She pulled the knob down one more notch. Nothing. A third notch. The car jerked forward. Even though her foot wasn't on the accelerator, it was moving. The front tires crunched over the gravel and rolled onto the smooth surface of the road.

Roy was still yelling, but Cheyenne ignored him. She concentrated on straightening out the car—driving only by sound—so that all four tires were on the road. Only then did she gingerly put her foot on the accelerator. She was too afraid to go fast. If she went off the road and ran into a tree, then Roy would be free to do whatever he wanted to her. Her left front tire chattered in gravel. She jerked the wheel, heard Roy curse on the other side of the window. When the right tire left the road, she corrected more gently.

Outside she could hear Roy's footfalls. First he was walking beside her, and then running. Each of his steps spurred her to press the pedal a millimeter farther down. When a tire left the road, she adjusted the steering wheel infinitesimally. And then Roy began to fall back.

Cheyenne was just starting to let herself hope when a new sound made her jump. It was the electronic shrill of a cell phone.

What should she do? She felt paralyzed. Who could be calling Roy? TJ? Jimbo? Some friend of Roy's? Whoever it was, she was sure the kind of people who would call Roy would not be the kind to come to her rescue. There was no point in answering it.

Without thinking about it, Cheyenne had lifted her foot off the accelerator. The car began slowing down until it was barely moving.

Then Cheyenne realized something. Once whoever was on the line hung up, she could use the phone to dial 9-1-1. But to do that, she had to find it.

As she was turning her head, trying to get a fix on the sound, the phone gave one last bleat and then stopped. The ringing seemed to have come from the floor of the car. Putting her foot on the brake, she began to rake her fingers through the crumpled papers that littered the floor. She found a wrench, a screwdriver, some tool she couldn't identify. Finally, her fingers closed around the phone. It was the same bulky phone Roy had handed her the day before.

She had just pressed the number nine when she heard another sound. Roy's footsteps. Running, but with an odd hitching gait. Listening to them, Cheyenne knew for sure that she *had* shot him. All the same, he was catching up with her.

She pressed the one key twice, then several buttons before she finally found the send key and heard the tones as it went through. Holding it between ear and shoulder—the bulky size was actually useful—she grabbed the steering wheel.

"Nine-one-one." A woman's voice.

The rock slammed down on the window again. Cheyenne thought she felt a tiny pebble of glass bounce off her cheek.

"I need the police. Oh, please hurry!" She began to inch the car forward again. But she knew she could never go fast enough.

"What is the nature of your emergency?"

The words ran out of her like water bursting from a dam. "My name's Cheyenne Wilder and I've been kidnapped and now I'm in a car and I've locked the doors but the kidnapper is outside and he's trying to smash open the window with a rock!"

"Does he have a weapon?" The woman's voice was still calm.

"Just the rock. But the window's starting to crack!"

"Do you have the keys?"

"Yes."

"Can you drive away?"

"I'm trying, but the thing is, I'm blind."

"Blind!" The dispatcher took a deep breath. "Okay, tell me where you are, Cheyenne."

"That's the thing. I don't know." This time when the rock crashed down, there was a splintery sound. The window *was* cracking. She had to get away. Cheyenne pressed the accelerator a little farther. The right front crunched on gravel. She adjusted, but not enough. The right rear tire had left the road as well. She angled away from the sound. "I'm somewhere within an hour's drive of the Woodlands Experience shopping center. I'm on a road next to some woods. It's paved and has gravel shoulders. And it's quiet. I've only heard one car in the past half hour."

"Okay, I can see which cell phone tower is relaying your call. That narrows it down—but not enough. We've still got a five-mile radius to cover. I'm alerting all units in your area to see if they can find you." Cheyenne heard her relay instructions.

Another blow smashed the window. Cracks spread, making a sound like cellophane uncrinkling.

"Cheyenne!" Roy howled. "Cheyenne!"

"Is that him?" A hint of shock crept into the dispatcher's carefully dispassionate voice.

"Yes!" Cheyenne panted. "Please hurry!"

"We're coming, Cheyenne."

After an endless stretch of time that was probably less than a minute, something wailed faintly in the distance. "Wait! I hear a siren!"

"From which direction? I've got four cars, but they are spread over a pretty wide area."

"I think south, but I'm not sure." Cheyenne thought of something. "Can you ask them to turn on their sirens one at a time?"

"Yes, but what—" and then understanding broke. "Yes! Hang on, I'll ask them to go one at a time. And you tell me which one you hear."

"Car one," the dispatcher said. Silence.

"Nothing," Cheyenne said. She was afraid she wouldn't be able to hear, so she lifted her foot from the accelerator.

With one hand, Cheyenne reached over and ran her fingers over the pane. It felt like a web of pebbles. The rock smashed down again just as she was touching the glass. And suddenly there was cold air pouring into the car. The hole was only as big as a dime, but she knew that wouldn't last.

"Car two."

"Still nothing." Cheyenne had never felt more alone in her life.

"Car three."

And finally she heard its wail.

"That's it! And it sounds closer than it did before."

"Got it!" the dispatcher said triumphantly. "We're coming!"

Then a hand punched through the window and circled her throat, squeezing Cheyenne back against the headrest. The phone fell to the floor of the car. Where was the gun? She didn't remember, and when she swept her hand over the seat, she couldn't find it. Roy's hand tightened. She couldn't scream—she couldn't even breathe—but she could hear the wail of the siren getting louder.

Scrabbling desperately, Cheyenne found the piece of glass in her pocket. She grabbed it—ignoring how it sliced her thumb—and dragged it across the back of his hand. Roy cursed, then let go of her throat and pried the piece of glass away from her. It was slick with blood, his and hers, and she couldn't hold on.

Then Roy's hand was back, like a steel band around her throat. She was going to die, just seconds before being rescued. No! No! She couldn't die. Not now. Maybe if she started driving again, he would have to let go. One hand found the wheel as her foot pressed the accelerator.

Then there was a thump and a scream, and Roy's hand was gone. And she felt the rear tire go over something.

Cheyenne heard a car screeching to a stop behind her. The siren cut out. Two doors were flung open.

A man's voice called out. "Stop! Police! Stay on the ground!"

Footsteps ran toward her. "Cheyenne, it's the police," a second man said. "You're safe now."

Cheyenne didn't move for a long moment. Then she said, "Let me feel your badge." Her foot was on the brake, but she could pivot it to the accelerator at any time.

"What?"

"Didn't they tell you I'm blind? Let me feel your badge. The man who just tried to kill me told me that he was a cop." Cheyenne held out her left hand next to the hole—but she kept her right hand on the steering wheel.

She heard him fumble and then he pressed the badge into her hand. Cheyenne ran her thumb across the raised letters. With a trembling hand, she turned off the engine.

"What took you so long?" she whispered.

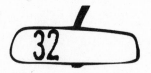

Just a Friend?

Two weeks later, the phone rang just as Cheyenne finished pouring hot water into her cocoa. She answered it.

"Hello?"

There was a silence at the end of the line. Then a voice said hesitantly, "Cheyenne?"

Suddenly, she was wide awake, even though she had only gotten four hours' sleep the night before. She was still having trouble sleeping.

"Who is it, Cheyenne?" Danielle called from the living room. Danielle and Cheyenne's dad were watching a football game.

"Just a second," Cheyenne said into the phone and then called out, "It's just a friend."

Leaving the cocoa on the counter, she walked down the hall to her room, and closed the door.

"What do you want?" She leaned her forehead against the cool wood of the door.

Griffin's voice was very soft. "I was calling to wish you a happy new year."

"How did you get my number?" Cheyenne realized she was trembling. Sensing her emotions, Phantom got up from his bed on the floor and rubbed against her thigh. She steadied herself by resting her hand on the back of his neck.

"You gave it to my dad, remember? Twice."

"Didn't you think I might be trying to forget?"

"I'm sorry." Griffin's voice suddenly sounded younger and much less certain. "I'll let you go."

Cheyenne didn't mean to say them, but the words burst out of her. "No—wait." She took a deep breath. "Are you calling from Chicago?"

"So you heard about that? Yeah, they put me with my mom's sister and her family. They say I met Aunt Debby when I was three, but I don't remember it. Nobody liked Roy much, so I guess my mom stayed away after that."

At the thought of Roy, Cheyenne felt her lip curl. "I guess they were right."

"Yeah." Griffin sighed. "I spent all those years thinking Mom must be mad at me. I still can't believe she's dead."

Cheyenne had heard about the deaths: Griffin's mom's seven years ago and then Jimbo's in the woods.

"Have you talked to your dad?"

Cheyenne couldn't stand to think of Roy. It worked only if she thought of him as Griffin's dad. She had run over his lower legs with her back tires, fracturing both of them. She had also shot him in the side, but the bullet had only grazed him, missing anything vital. Her dad had told Cheyenne that Roy had been charged with kidnapping, assault, and second-degree murder. Pending a mental health evaluation, TJ faced a dozen charges, including murder. Griffin had agreed to cooperate with authorities.

"No," Griffin said. "I'm not allowed to. In fact, they don't even know I'm calling you. I'm sure they would freak out if they knew we were talking."

"Ditto," Cheyenne said softly.

"I called from a pay phone in case your stepmom or dad answered. So they wouldn't see my aunt's name on the caller ID."

Cheyenne had tried to explain it to them, but it was clear that Danielle and Nick were more comfortable thinking of Griffin as the bad guy who had kidnapped their daughter. They didn't like to talk about how Cheyenne had done her best to kill Griffin or how he had saved her in the woods.

"Guess who's in our backyard right now?"

There was a pause, then Griffin said slowly, "You're not serious."

"Yeah, Duke. I begged my parents until they hired a dog trainer to find him in the woods and then work with him here. A woman. He still doesn't seem to like men very much."

Griffin gave a short laugh. "It's hard to think of Duke liking anyone."

After a pause, Cheyenne said, "So how's it going at your aunt's house?"

"To be honest, I kind of feel like Duke. They all watch me out of the corner of their eye. They've signed me up for this high school for alternative students. It sounds like it will be me and the pregnant girls and the kids with drug problems." But Griffin didn't sound bitter. "If I have to do it, I figured I might get some of those recordings you talked about. You know, of books. See if they would help me read."

"That's good," Cheyenne said. It was hard to talk. She had so many emotions, but they were mixed up so that she couldn't feel any one of them. "A new year, a new you," she said lightly.

"Hey, if Duke can do it . . . ," Griffin said. "How about you? Do you have any New Year's resolutions?"

"Just one. Always to take Phantom with me." Hearing his name, Phantom looked up and butted her thigh. Absently, she scratched him behind the ears.

"Everything would have been completely different if you had had your dog." It was hard to read what Griffin was feeling. Was he thinking about what he had learned about his dad? Or what he had learned about himself? Cheyenne knew that she would never be the same after what had happened.

"You're right. Things never would have turned out the way they did," Cheyenne said slowly. "But maybe that's okay."

"Cheyenne, are you about ready for lunch?" her dad called from the living room.

"Look, I've got to go," she said.

"Can I call you again?" Griffin said quickly.

Cheyenne took a deep breath and thought about her answer.

ACKNOWLEDGMENTS

I'd like to thank all the folks at Holt, but most especially my editor, Christy Ottaviano. Judy Watford generously shared her thoughts about being blind and even proofread the book by having her computer read it to her. Former Eugene high school student Leslie Elaine Weilbacher told me about her experiences, including how her guide dog, Cammy, changed her life. Robin Burcell, police investigator and author, pretty much knows everything and is always willing to share it. Portland 9-1-1 supervisor Todd DeWeese helped me with one final twist. And last but certainly not least, Malinda Carlson, Pacific Northwest field manager for Guide Dogs for the Blind, was beyond helpful.